HUSBAND
MEMORY
PICKLES

HUSBAND MEMORY PICKLES

&

Eleven Other Stories

DOUGLAS ATWILL

SUNSTONE PRESS

SANTA FE

Sunstone books may be purchased for educational, business, or sales promotional use.
For information please write: Special Markets Department, Sunstone Press,
P.O. Box 2321, Santa Fe, New Mexico 87504-2321.

Cover photograph by Douglas Atwill
Body typeface › Poliphilus MT Pro
Printed on acid-free paper
∞
eBook 978-1-61139-279-1

Library of Congress Cataloging-in-Publication Data
Atwill, Douglas.
[Short stories. Selections]
Husband memory pickles & eleven other stories / by Douglas Atwill.
      pages ; cm
ISBN 978-0-86534-999-5 (softcover : alk. paper)
I. Atwill, Douglas. Husband memory pickles. II. Title.
III. Title: Husband memory pickles and eleven other stories.
PS3601.T85A6 2014
813'.6--dc23

2014016482

WWW.SUNSTONEPRESS.COM
SUNSTONE PRESS / POST OFFICE BOX 2321 / SANTA FE, NM 87504-2321 /USA
(505) 988-4418 / ORDERS ONLY (800) 243-5644 / FAX (505) 988-1025

Contents

Husband
Memory
Pickles

She knew the tourists would arrive at her studio gallery early on this fine day, walking up to Canyon Road. Marian Nakamura painted small landscapes and gardens in the manner her father had taught her when she was a child in Osaka. She was pleased that a daughter could paint, perhaps as well as her father. Her canvases sold well over the years, paying for the gallery property and leaving a modest sum for her retirement years.

Nakamura had been a war bride who moved with her American sailor husband to his Santa Fe hometown at the end of the war. She painted and he opened a gallery, joining the art community, beginning a life together in the high altitude. He told her that he loved to watch her work, to see the magic unfold. When he died from a fall while picking pears from a high branch a few years later, she decided to remain in Santa Fe. To return home without a spouse could be seen as a loss of face, the faraway truth of her widowhood perhaps in question at home. She took back the Nakamura last name; those first years after her husband's death were possible only with her father's money from Osaka.

Painting filled her time, but her sadness lingered. After the September pears had fallen for several consecutive seasons, she finally stopped resenting the lethal tree. It was a waste to leave so many bruised pears on the ground for the night animals. Instead, remembering her family recipe for plums pickled in rice vinegar with mustard seed and caraway, Nakamura decided to use the fallen fruit. Her version with pear slices was piquant and crisp, redolent with floral overtones. She ordered square bottles and designed a label with the title Husband Memory Pickles. She arranged the slices in the Osaka way and sealed the bottles with red beeswax and braided raffia.

Visitors to her gallery were at first stand-offish about the pears, but one by one the first bottles disappeared, though often as mere gifts from Marian to the buyers of paintings. As the years passed her pickles grew popular, and tourists sometimes told her that they came to the gallery for the pickles as much as for her paintings. Her production grew to more than one hundred bottles each year.

More visitors from Japan started to find their way up Canyon Road to her gallery. Marian enjoyed returning their formal bows in the traditional way and hearing their soft-voiced questions about the pickles. A woman buyer from a Tokyo department store admired her bottles one day.

"May I have all the pickles, please?" the visitor asked, running her finger along the long shelf of bottles. Marian noticed how stylishly the woman was dressed, as if from New York rather than Japan.

"Would you like a painting, as well?" Nakamura asked.

"No, thank you."

"Perhaps this pen and ink drawing then?"

"No, again. But may we have all of next year's Memory Pickles, and the year after that? For the major downtown store only."

"Please leave your card and I will consider it."

It was now twenty years and several thousand pickles since her husband had taken his fall. She knew her paintings were better than ever, colors muted and complex in the particular way she saw the hills and trees around her. Had he lived her husband would have been so proud. Sometimes in the afternoons, she imagined he sat behind her, smiling. Now he seemed to be telling her to move on.

When the last person left that day, she closed the gallery and knew she would stop collecting the pears. It was time for a change if the bottles had become more important than her paintings. She lettered a new sign for tomorrow's tourists: No More Husband Memory Pickles.

The Cranbrook

She was the youngest of the four Babcock sisters from Stillwater, Minnesota. Her first name was Earmalinda, which when connected with the Babcock last name was a bumblesome mouthful that brought smiles to most people who heard it. She was a good daughter and suffered in silence, thinking how different life might have been as Elizabeth or Katherine.

Having graduated with good grades in fine arts from the university, she felt confident that she could always teach art. It was the fallback position that the Babcock parents stressed for all their daughters.

Earmalinda returned to Stillwater to teach at the Grover Cleveland High School. With the other sisters married off, living at home was comfortable. The large house on a double lot with shade oaks had come down to Mrs. Babcock through her family. Some neighbors thought that Mrs. Babcock had married down for love, to a much younger military man from the West Coast. Earnest Babcock had been twenty-two to her thirty-six. Her great-aunts referred to her as Our Poor Arthurine, undeserving of the grand mansion built by her lumber-baron grandfather, Jacob Lean, and inherited by her after his death. The great-aunts were left to divvy up his garnet stickpins and the twenty volumes of the Encyclopedia Britannica he had bequeathed them.

This was a time when most families in the Midwest had a store of unmarried aunts, their possible husbands having become one with the fields of France. These maiden ladies became librarians, bank tellers and minders of children. They served as a Greek chorus for the town, keeping alive common knowledge about family connections. Mrs. Babcock's great-aunts were kindly but rather too susceptible to a dark view of human nature. Gossip was the spine of their day.

The Lean Mansion that had eluded them was nonetheless a happy house and Earmalinda felt at ease there, refurnishing her childhood turret room with pieces suitable for a grown woman. On weekends and holidays she helped her father repair the mansions's trim, curlicues and carpenter-gothic fanlights. Her skill with tools was considered an adjunct to creative talent, as was her preference for trousers and baseball caps in her own hours.

Though her teacher's salary was low, it was ample for a young woman living at home. Her savings account at the Stillwater State Bank grew to a sum substantial enough to make her feel she could afford a car of her own.

At dinner one evening she brought up the matter. "What do think about my buying a car? No more worry about driving me to the school."

"Your father enjoys driving you, my dear," Mrs. Babcock said.

"But he's never liked being outside in Minnesota in December and January."

"That's true, a California boy at heart. What do you think, Earnest?"

He asked, "Can you afford it?"

Earmalinda said, "There's plenty in the bank. I could drive west on the summer vacation, see what's there."

"You're the best driver of all the girls—with a mind all your own," he said.

"Thank you, Papa. You can still take me to school in the warmer months, just as before."

Consensus was the Babcock way. None of them or the Leans (other than Jacob) discussed details about money, such as the actual amount Earmalinda might have in the bank. Mr. Babcock offered to go with her to the Plymouth dealership, but Earmalinda said she wanted to buy the car on her own. The family had always owned Plymouths—well-built, unpretentious machines—so he assumed she would continue along that line. Mr. Babcock wondered if she would choose a two-door or the more practical four-door sedan. There was no question about the color—silver gray was the color for the Babcocks.

But Earmalinda came back with a convertible-top coupe, a light canary yellow with a British tan cloth top. It was, indeed, a Plymouth, although chosen from the sportier pages of the company's catalog, a model named the Cranbrook. She parked it in the front driveway with a triple honk. Her mother watched from the porch with crossed arms, but Mr. Babcock was happy for his youngest girl as he and the neighbors inspected the white-wall wheels and bird's-eye maple steering wheel.

The great-aunts decided it was the purchase of this car that constituted the continental divide in Earmalinda's life. They had never entirely trusted Earnest, with his California ways, and now the same unsavory qualities were surfacing in his daughter.

Earmalinda, reading about modern art in Life Magazine, asked her students to draw inspiration from Picasso rather than from the traditional examples in their textbooks. They loved the new freedom, with paint dribbling down from women's heads with three eyes, fingers like sausages. Many of the boys, trying not to smile, drew large red testicles in their renditions of Spanish bull fights. The principal got word of the changes in the art curriculum, but she held back comment, thinking this was the new America. Grover Cleveland students, just like those from the large city schools, needed to be prepared for anything that came their way.

Miss Babcock's art courses became most popular, while woodworking and homemaking suffered. The school year concluded with Earmalinda pleased but wondering what to do with her summer months. However, a chance question by one her students kept coming back to her.

"Do you paint like Picasso, Miss Babcock?" he asked.

"I don't know who I paint like, Harold."

"Will you bring one of your paintings for the class to see?"

She patted his arm and said, "As soon as I finish one."

If an art teacher does not paint, can she truly be an artist? Earmalinda needed to start painting herself, if for no other reason than for Harold. She searched for the advertisement she remembered in an art teacher's journal. There it was.

Three Weeks in Santa Fe
PLEIN AIR DE-MYSTIFIED
Open-air classes with
A Master Instructor
Hotel Room and Breakfast included.
$350.

Earmalinda wrote a check and mailed it off. She would spend July in Santa Fe, learning how to paint a landscape outside, bringing back canvases for Harold and the others to critique. It would also give the Cranbrook its first real outing, a chance to blow out the soot.

As Arthurine and Earnest watched from the front porch, she backed out the drive, promising to write. It was a three-day journey across the plains and down into New Mexico, and the temperature gauge almost topped out as she crested La Bajada Hill approaching Santa Fe. There it was off at the end of the trail, with squat brown buildings and centuries-old trees pushing against the foothills.

On her drive from Stillwater, she thought about what kind of paint-ing she wanted to attempt. Although Matisse moved on from his Fauvist beginnings, she had always turned with delight back to those early images. The old painter had given up too soon, not exploring all the possibilities. Fauvism was an idea she wanted for herself.

The "Master Instructor" was a Hungarian exile named Anton who each summer gave six *plein air* classes, which, coupled with the sales of his own paintings to the suggestible students, gave him enough for a full year's residence in Santa Fe. Anton appeared to favor Earmalinda, and his lanky frame stood more often beside her easel than the others. He quickly recognized the source of her disjointed lines and large splotches of color.

12

"Matisse, Derain—not bad. Here and here are wrong. Don't stop the color before the edge."

"Are the shapes wrong?" she asked.

"And your colors. Keep working."

She mastered the look if not the Matissean genius of Fauvism by the end of the first week. As the students moved about the town for a change of motif, resident artists and townspeople came by to see what was on their easels. The response to Earmalinda's canvases was enthusiastic and she received several purchase offers.

Anton suggested a price of twenty-five dollars, and just to encourage her, as a mentor should, said he might buy a few himself. He made a sour face when she said she wanted to keep them. How could she return to Stillwater without hard evidence for Harold that she had changed from a chrysalis to a butterfly?

Anton saw Earmalinda as quite different from the ordinary workshop student. By the closing week, she had honed in on her landscapes, concentrating the bands and lines of color to make them sing. Orange trunks vibrated in front of sea green mountains with a watermelon sky holding it all together. Anton had struggled for years to reach his plateau, and now this young Minnesota woman was firmly encamped on hers in just a few weeks. Unlike the other amateurs, with their murky colors and hesitant lines, she could not put down a wrong brushstroke. It might behoove him to make her a proposition, one that would be profitable for him as well. She was packing up the Cranbrook for her return trip.

"Earmalinda, my dear, I have something to say before your return to Samewater."

"Stillwater, Anton."

"Ah, well. I know you are committed to teaching, but you must come back to Santa Fe next year for the entire summer. Your lust for color is alive, spread across the surface of each canvas. You have the eye, you know, and could well paint in three months a hundred or so paintings—very saleable paintings."

"Maybe. It seems right for me."

"I will sponsor you in a downtown gallery, act as your agent. September is the month for exhibits, well-dressed people are in town for the autumn color."

"Where would I stay?"

"I have the fine spare room. You could come and go, as you like. If I am to be your agent, there would be no charge whatsoever. *Sans souci.*"

"That's generous, Anton. Let me think about it. On the drive back."

"Just to put a number on it, the hundred paintings might retail for a three hundred dollars each. Half would be yours, the rest for the gallery and a mere bit for me. Fifteen thousand dollars, all for you—perhaps sniggling up the prices toward the end, to rake in a bit more."

"So much? More than my annual salary in just three months?"

"Say the word. You must, of course, leave a few of your better pieces with me to lay before the eyes of the galleries, to do my magic."

Earmalinda tried to allay her suspicions about Anton, including what portended with his roving hand while she stood at the easel. Several times he had caressed her buttocks, with a covert giggle. There were many other parts of his new proposal that could go wrong. She was about to mention a few when Anton interrupted.

"A generous advance would not be out of the question. Say a two-thousand dollar check today. A simple assent from you. I know from watching you that once you set your sights, the target is doomed."

"Let me write you back."

"Very well. But, let it be yes."

"Thank you, Anton."

"One more thing. Minnesota is not a proper place for an artist such as you, and teaching is not your path. Painting is." If Anton was a sexual rascal and financial scoundrel, a part of him was a true artist with a kindness that often undermined his more nefarious schemes. Earmalinda heard that part and decided it would not hurt to leave three canvases, just to see what would happen. There would still be twelve to show to her fall classes. Anton

14

picked his three and clutched them under one arm as he waved goodbye with the other. Earmalinda realized that the art world had truly beckoned, pulling away a curtain that exposed both the pleasures and the pitfalls of its curving passageways.

For the remainder of the summer back in Minnesota, she carried the French easel around the town and its outskirts to paint hometown scenes. She had hoped to prove Anton wrong, to show him that art can grow large anywhere. Neighbors gazed in perplexed silence and awkward smiles when she turned to look at them. This was unlike the open adoration that she earned in Santa Fe. Fauvism and Stillwater might never mix. Her home lacked the dark delight of New Mexico, where odd patches of Fauvist color actually existed, right there for the looking. She wrote Anton asking if the two-thousand dollar advance still stood.

When the school year started she hung her dozen paintings across the walls of her classroom. Harold looked at each of them solemnly, his nose a few inches away. Earmalinda could almost see the gears grinding in his head as he tried to understand why he ought to consider these paintings good. She noted that he had nearly grown into a man and was the tallest of the class, with a curious mix of a boy's wonderment stretching to fill a man's demeanor.

He stayed after class to ask, "Can I be an artist?"

"I don't see why not."

"Can I make a living at it? Dad says I should switch to machine shop—they always want machinists."

"He's right, Harold. Art is not really needed."

"But you're needed. And making a living."

"Just barely. Don't forget I have free room and board at home."

"Will people buy your paintings?"

"There's a man in Santa Fe who thinks they will."

"If they were mine, I would keep them all, never let them go."

Was Harold getting too fond of the teacher? Earmalinda made a note to watch out—she must not bring hurt to her students, especially this most alert and responsive among them. If she played down the glamour and importance of art, it might be better.

She brought up the topic of a full Santa Fe summer with her father while they were burning the piles of oak leaves that had required a full Saturday morning to collect.

"Do you like my paintings, Papa?"

"I love you, sweetheart, and that's all that matters."

"So, I guess you don't. There's no reason anyone in Stillwater should like them. Mrs. Billows down the block almost laughed out loud when she looked over my shoulder."

"Why do you ask?"

"I want to paint more. In Santa Fe, because nothing good happens when I paint here."

"Move away to New Mexico?"

"Only for the summer. The full three months. Anton promises an exhibit of whatever I can finish. Maybe you and Mama can drive out for a week or two."

"So far away when I ought to hoe the corn every week."

"I understand."

He looked away as he said, "Are we losing you? Your mother thinks so."

Earmalinda kissed her father on the cheek, the Babcock way of not answering a difficult question.

Anton's check arrived in late November, along with a letter. He had made a list of wonderful new changes for her to consider, ideas that would make her paintings fly off the walls of the gallery. He would disclose them in person, next June. And when June arrived, she left Stillwater for Santa Fe once again.

Thus the painting summer of Earmalinda Babcock began. However, the thought of Anton's spare room had made her uneasy, so she instead rented a place with the Martinez family on Delgado Street. Out and about with her easel every day, she waited until the end of the second week to

16

show Anton what she had painted—ten canvases in her increasingly adept technique, a neo-Fauvism.

The pictures were all painted from a site by the river, a small cascade in the midst of willows, sienna-hued outcroppings and young cottonwoods. The New Mexico sun made dark purple shadows and the highlights burned almost white, with pale oranges and violets almost asking to be included.

"Your touch you haven't lost," Anton said.

"Would you join me tomorrow?" she asked, hoping the camaraderie of side-by-side easels in the landscape would soothe his annoyance at her having largely ignored him. It would be fellow painters against the world.

"There's an afternoon class, but tomorrow morning would be good."

"The apple orchard off the Camino?"

"Fine. Glad you're back."

By the end of the first month she had patched things up with Anton and finished thirty paintings, with some new motifs. From the shelter of a neighbor's portal, she painted three versions of afternoon rainstorms, angled blue lines crashing through deep green foliage. Morning sun became her favorite subject, as she converted tree trunks and branches to strong red and orange lines. Anton often painted with her, but he could not keep up with her pace and originality. All traces of his former irritation faded as he watched, and he referred to Earmalinda everywhere as his protégée. Anton canceled his remaining *plein air* classes to pinpoint his focus on her. There was no recurrence of his wandering hand nor the snicker.

By July there were often several onlookers watching Earmalinda from folding chairs in the nearby shade. Anton deserted his easel to regale them about what Earmalinda was doing, how she had singlehandedly resurrected the moribund ideas of Fauvism, bent them to work for her. It was as if she had channeled a young Matisse or Vlaminck to guide her hand.

Earmalinda seldom listened to the palaver Anton was spouting as her concentration mostly blocked out his words. For Anton it was groundwork for her September exhibit as he prepared to fill the role of persuader, beguiler, and shill.

He said one morning, "You don't mind my talking to others about your work, do you, my dear?"

"No, Anton. I need to stay at the easel—not talk to people."

"Exactly. While I start the rhythm of the waves."

"I have overheard your remarks, though. I could barely recognize myself."

"Goddess-making is like sausage-making."

"I should not listen?"

"Wise girl. Let the high priest do his embroidery."

"I have a question, Anton. About your list of changes."

"Simple, obvious things, really. Like your name."

"Earmalinda?"

"So unfortunate. Why don't we shorten it to Malin? Euphonious, rolling off the tongue. No need anymore to stumble."

"What else?"

"Let your hair grow a bit before September. Too much like a boy's now."

"And...?"

"That cap and those jeans. A nice silk dress to show off your breasts would be so much more compelling. I have a stylish woman friend who can advise us."

Earmalinda waited a while before responding. "If I don't agree?"

"No matter. You merely endanger your own sales, your own career— my entire life."

"All this to make the paintings fly off the walls?"

"They won't on their own take flight, my dear."

The legend that might become Earmalinda Babcock was coalescing. Whether protégée or spiritual daughter in Anton's lectures, Earmalinda was in truth leaping ahead in dexterity and inventiveness.

The bright colors became muted, like seventh and ninth chords in music, colors vibrating against each other with an agreeable dissonance. The last paintings of the summer were songs of great strength, containing opposite colors in perfect balance. Her hand was so unerring that Earmalinda had several times wondered if Anton's nonsense about channeling might not contain a kernel of truth.

At August's end there were eighty paintings in Earmalinda's room at the Martinez house, leaning in stacks face to the wall. Anton had wanted to have them framed in advance of the show as they were produced, a few at a time, eager to proceed to the selling part of their contract. Earmalinda put him off.

"I want to see them all together, like a school choir on the graduation bleachers," she told him.

"Don't be too long."

"Only a few days—to know that this is really the end of the project."

"I can't wait to see them on the gallery walls with their splendid colors. To hear the pop of champagne corks and the spontaneous applause, to see the green eyes of the other painters."

"Cool down, Anton."

"I'm so happy I feel like a little boy," he said, flailing his arms about like a gawky student.

But Earmalinda ran away that night, packing the Cranbrook in stealth, driving off without the headlights. She left a letter refunding Anton's two thousand dollars and asking him to forgive her. He could be her sole agent now, deciding how to sell the paintings and for what price. Senora Martinez was keeping them safe for him, but there was one missing, on its way back for a certain student in Stillwater. Please mail her share of sales when everyone decided what it was. Goodbye for now.

Anton made great hay out of her departure, saying she had vaporized into the sky like the delicate summer rain. Perhaps a Portuguese nunnery was her hiding place or a secret assignment in Asia for the Foreign Service. There may never be another brilliant reincarnation from the most exciting of the French decades. Knowing this, he parceled out the paintings for the September exhibit, only a few dozen at first. More were rumored to be in the vaults at the First National Bank, safe for posterity. He foresaw a comfortable future for himself, bringing a few out at a time, each occasion warranting a handsome rise in price. Since he did not share the address of the Lean Mansion in Stillwater with others, he could forestall any individual communication with his protégée.

Earmalinda settled back into her turret room and the school year at Grover Cleveland. Arthurine and Earnest were delighted to have her back. Both felt that there was a sense of waiting in their youngest daughter and that the artistic west would call her back in the end. She had come home for a while to make them happy, the dutiful youngest daughter. When she was away from the house, they talked about how it was only a matter of time before the yellow Cranbrook disappeared around the corner. Santa Fe had made changes in her, subterranean changes they did not understand. Both of them sensed a yearning in their daughter. How could art have a call so strong?

Earmalinda and Earnest were raking leaves again, the piles growing as they enjoyed being together without words. Since direct communication was difficult for all the Babcocks, silence often held sway at the Mansion. Ideas could build up until they could not wait any longer, this time breaking out in Earnest first.

He said, "Your mother and I are so happy to have you back. Happy that Santa Fe did not steal you away"

"Thanks, Papa."

"She wanted me to tell you—your sisters have their own homes, but you always have a place here with us, no matter what."

"That makes me feel safe."

"Do you have plans?"

"I'm just going to wait until something good happens."

"Something will."

"I know, Papa. I know."

If the summer saw an explosive bloom in Earmalinda as a young artist, it also saw a matching physical upwelling in Harold, who was two inches taller and as much broader in the shoulders. Despite his new height, he gave her an open, boyish smile when she presented him with the single painting from the west. He said he would keep it right next to his bed, where he could see it the last moment before sleep and again in the first morning light.

Earmalinda watched him as the year proceeded, and the one after that, not looking with a direct gaze, but still seeing his Nordic features turn from the innocence of a blond colt to the allure of a golden man, an amiable lad become full-sized man. It would not be much longer now, the summer harvest of a fully ripe plum. Earnest and Arthurine would learn soon how unlike her sisters their youngest daughter was, headstrong and eccentric, and the great-aunts could never have imagined what a glorious few years they were about to have, their phones ringing and ringing and ringing with outrage.

Grinding Corn

Now in her early thirties, Sarah McIntosh waited in the office adjoining the studio of her father, the painter Palestine McIntosh. The room had a desk, a chair and a small sofa, with filing cabinets along a sidewall. Above the sofa hung three of Palestine's paintings, pueblo views with high mountains and banks of storm clouds above. Although the landscapes were part of his oeuvre, he was known nation-wide for his paintings of nude pueblo maidens, often asleep in the folds of striped rugs. He had done over a hundred versions of the motif, most of them bursting with color and strong shadow. Every month, calls from art collectors came into Sarah's office seeking news of a possible new painting.

As the studio manager, Sarah was in charge of interviewing and hiring her father's models. A young woman had called earlier in the morning responding to her newspaper ad: *Wanted - Female model to pose nude for celebrated painter, 292-2222.* She told Sarah that she would walk out from town for the interview. As the road was steeper and more difficult than people expected, prospective models tended to arrive late and exhausted. Sarah brought a book to read while she waited. The model was now forty minutes overdue.

There was a soft knock. Sarah opened the door and beckoned the somewhat breathless woman inside. Sarah noted that she was nevertheless in better shape than most applicants who arrived on foot wet and panting.

"I'm sorry about the hill. I should describe it in the ad. Please take off your coat and sit down," Sarah said, motioning to the sofa.

She watched as the girl untied the belt of her cloth coat. It was a good omen that her first moves were graceful, measured and spare, without fidgeting or nerves. She took off the coat, folded it neatly and sat down beside it.

"What is your name, please?" Sarah asked.

"Poti Nadoon."

"Is that an actual native American name?"

"No."

"Is it Asian?"

"No."

"It could be Middle Eastern, I suppose."

"No."

"Well, then, what is it?"

"Poti is a very old name, Nadoon is my mother's family."

"Where from?"

"I've been living on the East Coast."

"I meant where is your name from?"

"I know."

Sarah realized that she could not pry out the information she sought. It did not matter where Poti's name came from, only what she looked like. None of the painter's other models had been of Native American stock. Several had been from Poland, one from the highlands of China and another from coastal Mexico. At the local pueblos, the real pueblo maidens were warned off removing their clothes for strangers, no matter how august or talented. Sarah had come to think that this forbidden touch was one of the main reasons the portraits were so well received by collectors.

Palestine's last model had married a local sculptor who did not want her to work in the nude anymore. In the months following the painter had been working on landscapes, and was now keen to get back to the human figure, asking Sarah more often about her interviewing progress.

In these interludes between paid models, Sarah often asked if she could pose for her father, but he always found a reason to say no. *Your hips are too narrow, dear,* or *you've grown much too pretty and tall,* or *you know*

I ask for a tawny skin tone, or *I think the art world expects a younger body.* She learned that a daughter cannot be all things to a father, however much she wants to please. She stopped asking to be the focus of his eye, trying to be content as a helpmate.

Sarah said to Poti, "No matter about your name. Please stand up and turn around."

Poti rose from the sofa in a smooth move, stood facing Sarah for a few moments and turned her profile. Then, without prompting, she offered her back and her other profile. She rearranged her arms with each move, ending with her hands on her waist. By then, Sarah knew that Poti would be perfect for the job.

"Please sit again. This position is for a nude model. You will need to pose with grace, not changing your stance. It will be necessary to sit, stand or lie down for hours, as my father paints with a slow brush. His works are in museums and are prized by collectors on both coasts. You will, of course, have no legal rights to the images. Is this all agreeable to you?"

"Yes. Do you want me to take my clothes off now?"

"No, Father must have the final say."

Sarah told her that she would be paid ten dollars an hour, would work every morning except Sundays, from eight to noon with a break until two. She would be welcome to eat lunch with the McIntosh family if she wished. A daybed was provided in the studio changing room for her to nap if she chose. There could be more hours in the afternoon if the painting was going well. She would be paid at the end of every week in cash. A selection of robes was available in the changing room, which had a bathroom adjoining.

There was no question in Sarah's mind that Palestine McIntosh would select Poti Nadoon as his new pueblo maiden model. She had the appealing mixture of modesty and boldness that Palestine always found irresistible. She also had the thick straight hair, black eyes, round face and, underneath her cotton dress, the wide hips and ample breasts that had become hallmarks of his maiden paintings.

Palestine included objects from his collection of tribal crafts in the corners of his canvases, as if the maiden might grow tired while grinding corn and fall asleep on a pile of blankets. Or as if she might put aside her bead-working frame to curl up in the warmth of a beaver throw, a narrow band of sunlight coursing up and across her torso. Each painting told a different story, but in all of them a maiden filled the design with her drowsy curves, often exhibiting the sensual insolence that was so much a trademark of McIntosh depictions.

"When can you start?"

"Tomorrow?"

"Very good. I'll see if father can see you now."

Sarah knocked once on the door and opened it. Palestine was standing at the easel next to a large studio window, working on a canvas of a poplar-strewn hill.

"Yes, Sarah?"

"Poti Nadoon is here. I think we've found a new model."

Palestine put his brush down and walked to the door. He stooped slightly to miss the low lintel, which had never been a friend to his tall frame. Sarah stood back to let him view the young girl. He shook Poti's hand, enveloping it in both of his.

"What a lovely name. Come in, my dear young Poti Nadoon."

Sarah saw the joy on his face, the way his eyelids narrowed momentarily, as he guided her in, hand on her back and closed the door. It was most unusual that family was invited into his studio when Palestine was working and never when he began a new canvas. It was a secret, creative space, away from the others.

Her morning's task completed, Sarah walked up the hill to the main house, where her mother would be preparing the family's lunch. If Sarah herself could not be a pueblo maiden, Sarah still deemed herself a vital servant to the noble cause, a vestal at the high altar of art. She knew there could be no maiden paintings without her efforts. The unclean feeling lasted only a moment.

The Dairymaids' Heads

It was not considered impolite at the time to ring up a fellow painter asking to see his current work and to make comments on the direction he had taken, supporting in this candid manner the cause of art. My friend Alfred Bruss and I made a point to do this every month or so, to assess what was going on in the private studios of the Santa Fe hills. Bruss's ex-wife, Zorina, passed around the unkind story that the two of us were really nosy old women in disguise, Miss Marples done up in denim. Zorina held her sharpened grudges close to the bosom, ready for immediate use.

Bruss and I took turns making the calls, as we each had a different list of painter acquaintances who might be disposed to see us. This way both of us gained access to studios we ordinarily did not see, as well as the opportunity to spread around the goodwill that we thought was becoming so scarce in our art community.

On his morning rounds Bruss came by my studio, where the new canvas of daffodils was not going well, and we were finishing off the pot of coffee before it attained its full bitterness. He asked, "What do you think of Penelope Goodge? I saw a painting of hers at the bank, on the wall at the trust department where we both have accounts. I was favorably impressed—a still life with strong lines, good brushwork, no fuzzy backgrounds."

"Do you want to give her a call?" I asked.

"I thought we might go by and see her new work, if you're so inclined."

"Let's do. I need to wait anyway for this yellow bit to dry."

"I know nothing about her personally, mind you, but we have talked while waiting for the trust officers. She's odd, but pleasant."

"How is she odd?"

"Tall—well over six feet. Piles of red hair, two Irish wolfhounds that never leave her side. Now that I think about it, not so very odd after all."

Bruss had written her telephone number on a card, which he took out and used to dial from my studio phone. She would see us right away as she had plans for an early lunch. Bruss got the directions to her studio, off an eastside street. The drive took only a few minutes and at the very end of the narrow lane we parked in front of an adobe ruin, an old house behind a high wall with brick parapets in disrepair. Small trees were growing right out of the wall and after opening the complaining entry gate we could see the house was in a similar state.

Sections of stucco had fallen away, exposing the courses of raw adobe bricks, and broken windowpanes were taped up with brown paper. The paving on the walkway was in disarray from rampant creepers, and the path itself was overgrown with unpruned viburnums and mock oranges. I could hear Bruss, whose studio resembled a Swiss surgery, clucking under his breath as he rapped the oversize dolphin knocker on the front door. Deep throated barking commenced far inside and got closer and closer.

Goodge opened the door as she held back the hounds with an outstretched arm. "They're perfectly safe, but don't let them slip by. We were all morning hunting them down yesterday. They are coursing dogs, you know."

As the barking subsided, Bruss did the introductions and Goodge invited us to follow her farther into the building to the actual studio. We walked down the wide hallway, across the end of a dining room, through a small library and into a high-ceilinged room with skylights and a tall studio window facing into a walled courtyard. Despite his Alpine tidiness, Bruss and I shared a deep love for the old houses of the historic district, so I did not need to look his way to know his full appreciation of the elegant seediness of the well-proportioned rooms. From the street, you might expect that a

Miss Havisham lived inside, but Goodge was a modern woman dressed in magenta trousers and a striped man's shirt with the tails out.

She said, "This was an old landscape painter's studio. I bought the house from his widow ten years ago and had no heart to change a thing. My sisters despair, but it suits me, even the leaks in the roof." She motioned towards construction buckets nearly full of water in the middle of the room.

Bruss got things going. "I've admired your painting of loaves of bread at the trust department," he said. "Strong design, bold color, well conceived."

"Thank you. From a group I finished last fall. I gained ten pounds with all the buttered warm slices, so no more loaves for a while. Would you like to see what I'm working on now?"

Bruss assented and she crossed over to canvases leaning against the wall. They were six-foot square panels, so Bruss helped her raise and turn the first one onto the easel. We stood back to look.

"I call this 'Mother's Buffet Plates,' one of a new series."

Neither Bruss nor I mustered anything to say as we studied a painting of broken china spread across a dark brick floor, plates and saucers all in shards. The scale was larger than life size, with pieces trailing off in splatter patterns as if the plates had been thrown down with great force. I recognized the blue and white designs of Meissen, a favorite of the older women in my family. A strong low light raked across the painting from one direction, bringing the broken curves high above their shadows, and a fainter red glow washed them from the opposite side, giving a devilish quality to the whole canvas. I was reminded of a crime scene photograph, perhaps just as Goodge intended.

"Mother was horrid," she said. "No proper childhood for any of us. She turned away every one of my boy friends, even the more suitable ones."

"This should do the trick, then," Bruss said. He was quicker-witted in these studio situations than I.

"Can't tell you how my spirits lifted. Minor ailments gone for good. Let me show you the other paintings."

Bruss helped her raise to the easel five more paintings of the same size, one after the other. Mother's Soup Tureen, Mother's Good Tea Cups, Mother's Breakfast Plates, Mother's Collection of Dairymaid Creamers and Mother's Pots-de-Crème. Light came from a different source in each painting, as if a whole day had been spent in an anti-Meissenry convulsion. The detail work was impressive—dangerous sharp edges against smooth porcelain surfaces. The dairymaids' heads were all together, like guillotined aristocrats. If good art has an underlayment of obsession, this was very good art, indeed. Despite herself, perhaps the mother had passed along something worthwhile to an unhappy daughter.

"Stunning work, Penelope," I said.

"I'm stopping with these. My sisters want me to continue on with the luncheon Wedgwood, but I feel the old girl's had enough. No clean flesh left to bruise."

"What's next?" Bruss asked.

"I've been dreaming about oranges on crumpled white linen. Some sliced, others piled up, peelings here and there, bees flying about."

"Like Zurbaran?"

"Messier than him, sticky juice everywhere. I'll ask you both over when I have them under way, but now I've got to change for my ladies' lunch. Thanks for coming by."

Having ended our interview with aplomb, she walked us to the front door, the dogs sniffing at our ankles. Bruss backed the car around and we headed to my studio.

"Did you dislike your parents?" Bruss asked.

"Not like that. The sheer hate."

"I guess we can't imagine the intensity of the mother-daughter thing."

"Father-son has its moments, but nothing so savage as the female version."

The rest of that day the broken china canvases kept coming back to my mind—how successful they were in dispelling the strangle hold of severe family hatred. I could see how the power of mother had been undone, defused. Goodge appeared to be truly free of her mother's grasp. I wondered if the mother in question were still alive and tried to remember if Goodge had spoken of her in the past tense.

I felt a growing envy of Goodge's gift for using her art as a weapon, particularly against one who was not there to fight back, like a child throwing a rock and running away. If the other Goodges had the same mania for revenge, what a counterattack mother might launch.

With blue and white china still on my mind, I had a restless night. After several short episodes of troubled sleep, I woke as the sun came up with a newborn resolve. I would turn my own long-held unhappiness with my father into art that would set me free. Just as Goodge had.

As I ate the breakfast that would give me fuel for the task—eggs, bacon, English muffins, marmalade and a dish of blueberries in cream—difficulties became apparent.

There was nothing about my distracted, cool father that I could throw on the floor, rearrange and make into art. How does one fight a passive, disinterested person, dead for twenty years, whose major sins had been those of omission: not loving enough, not being there, seldom touching, never giving approval, never communicating, looking away when I smiled? His trial at a celestial family court would find father innocent, guilty only of failing, and would reveal me as a demanding, fussy ingrate. Nevertheless, I headed to the studio.

I would start with a sketchbook. Pulling down a fresh one from the shelf, I hoped something would come to me as I drew. My first sketches were loose portraits from memory—father walking the family spaniel, father reading in a chair, lying down, sleeping, adjusting his gray suit, shooting dove in his hunting outfit, in the bathtub with a back brush, next to the family sedan, standing next to mother in a stiff formal pose on the front lawn of a farmhouse.

An idea about execution grew into more detailed drawings. A pin-stripe-suited father, blindfolded, against a bullet-pocked wall. A version of father hanging on the scaffold I tore out and crumpled up as too gruesome.

The electric chair scene got too busy with sockets and extension cords to afford a clear view of father behind the straps. Then I laughed out loud as I drew him as a bespectacled bureaucrat walking the plank for the amusement of taunting pirates. The design opportunities in the swirling flames distracted me from achieving a believable burning of father at the stake, bound together with some middle managers in an auto-da-fé of his peers. I liked the idea of a group execution, multiple fathers getting their reward, but seven fathers together in a gas chamber were too reminiscent of the last world war, so I crumpled them, too.

I broke for lunch, my drawing fingers strained from so many hours of reprisal. I had an inkling of awareness at how satisfied Goodge must have felt during her own artistic catharsis. Other colorful ideas flowed in like insistent ocean breakers as I sat eating at the kitchen table, so I pushed away the other half of the sliced-chicken sandwich with sweet pickles and mayonnaise, eager to return to my sketchbook. If I could leave food uneaten, what I was doing must be right.

Back in the studio, I drew father on a small raft, adrift on the sea because of his many crimes. Father next stood on an arctic ice floe while black-eyed white bears circled in the distance. He was stranded on a tropical sandbar encircled by shark fins, ship sailing away, and left to consider his deficiencies. Never a natural swimmer, father would not escape the alligators in a swampy scene replete with fully opened water lily blossoms and cypress roots. Father and his horse galloped away from a pyroclastic flow, searing hot clouds at their heels.

I noted that my drawing was getting better as I went on. Contorted positions were easier to render and I thought father's image grew harsher, more intrinsically evil, as the afternoon wore on. I could well be back in art school, rushing to finish an assignment to replicate the whiplash line of Aubrey Beardsley. I could almost hear the professor saying, what a refined Gothic touch you have, young man.

In the sketch of father as Icarus falling in a cascade of white feathers, I got too distracted in the tracery of the swirling, circling feathers. Then came father in a priest's habit, thrown over the mesa edge by pueblo women. Father hit by lightning, his briefcase exploding. Father taken away by a cyclone, holding onto his hat. Still clutching his briefcase, father carried off in the talons of a great bird, the family below nonchalantly eating dry cereal. Quicksand was a thought. I could see the classic outreach of the hand, nobody nearby to help, a disinterested crow on a high branch cleaning its feathers.

I was feeling so much better. Maybe this project would work, shrinking the jagged scar that I still harbored as an adult. I actually started to feel sorry for father. What a mean-spirited and ungrateful son I had become! Despite this first kernel of guilt, I had a notably untroubled night of rest. Murdering father had not murdered sleep.

The next morning Bruss called.

"I can't get Goodge's paintings out of my mind," he said.

"Me either."

"Her mother cut into small ribbons."

"I'm still amazed at the power of a simple idea."

"So I'm getting back at Zorina, and all unpleasant women, with my own painting."

"Me, too."

"I didn't know you ever had a wife."

"Of course not, Bruss. I'm drawing revenge sketches of my father."

"Back to it, then. Call me when you're clear."

The first sketchbook filled and I started another. New images flowed from my pen of father drowning, burning, beheaded, choking on a morsel of steak, falling from a plane, tripping down the Spanish Steps, tumbling off a fire-escape, falling through thin ice into a pond, and a dozen more.

Some civilized part of my brain then came foreword, not the reptilian lobe that had been having such a colorful spree. This part said the mayhem and bloodshed were taking up too much time, wasting ink and paper. It was a fool's mission, no matter if I felt liberated and cleansed. Father had done all he could. I needed to get back to the placid, Mannerist garden paintings

that had become so much a part of my days, to stop this vengeance by sketchbook. Blackness and bile needed to cease.

Penelope Goodge could excoriate her mother in oils, but I would
never be able to prolong this intensity long enough to finish a canvas. I was
flagging after a mere two days, lucky to have my line drawings. Maybe men
have no stomach for the long-term settling of scores. We are the weak knees
on the Greek stage, never to rise to the power of Medea howling across the
centuries. In two days we give up, whining and complaining of sore fingers.
At least I did.

I spent the remainder of the afternoon on the very last drawing. It was
an overgrown graveyard with a massive white headstone, birds perching on
its cornice, yew and boxwood pressing close. Around the perimeter of the
stone I drew a border of the roses, lilies, lavender, variegated leaves and the
curling tendrils that had become so much a part of my work. I filled the
center with a wide wreath of incised flowers, berries, buds and corymbs,
small insects crawling along the leaves. With long-serif italics I lettered *Rest
in Peace, Papa* in the circle and, after waiting a few minutes for the ink to
dry, put the sketchbooks back on the shelf, between the red leather one from
a hiking trip to the central backwoods of Turkey and the many Belgian
linen-covered ones of my summer gardens.

Cathedral Morning

The snow started at daybreak, deeply covering the skylight in David Deerfield's studio, darkening his easel. These were the joy-laden days of the Santa Fe Christmas season, with farolitos, luminarias, *bizcochitos*, and endless good cheer. He switched on the table lamps around the room, but they emitted barely enough light for him to get started. The large canvas on his easel, a commissioned portrait of the Cathedral, had been an uphill effort from the start. This diminished light would only add to the difficulties.

Deerfield had painted the cathedrals of South America and Europe, but his paintings of the St. Francis Cathedral were what had made his reputation. Many private collections in town included a Deerfield version of the stone basilica: in a winter storm, in a summer rain, under a rainbow, at night with stars, looked at from the clouds above or from beneath its upward-tapering towers. The images were now so numerous that he had decided to retire the motif, having nothing more to say.

On the day that Mrs. Willa Reilly, a rich, devout widow and the biggest contributor for the bronze fountain in the Cathedral's north garden, asked Deerfield to paint the edifice once again, he replied, "What if I painted the old adobe version instead, the one that stood there in the seventeenth century on the day before The Rebellion?"

She waved her hand at a nearby chair for him to sit. "It's the St. Francis Cathedral I want, my dear, not some politically correct statement about the past. I don't relish your pueblo people's revolt hovering over my buffet table, mixing in with the beaten biscuits and Virginia ham."

"But I'm sure I can paint the light of that August day, as it must have been before the events," Deerfield said.

"Forget about it. Adobe churches melt away. Give me good, solid buildings, stone buildings. The St. Francis."

"Stone also melts, Willa. The Temple of Artemis, wonder of the ancient world, is now a field of small pebbles on the Turkish coast. Goats pluck at the grasses."

"You think too much, David. Just get to work and paint what I want," she said, adjusting the tortoise-shell comb in her abundant, salt-and-pepper hair. She wrote out a deposit check and stood up, the interview over.

"Could I include just a hint about the frailty of man?" he asked. "A *Memento Mori?*"

"Do as you wish, but I want to see *my* St. Francis cathedral, in its glory. No funny business. No small touches of an uprising in the corners."

In the days that followed, Deerfield made a start, blocking in the major shapes. In spite of her warning, he definitely planned to include something unusual, a different slant on the old church. That something would present itself as he painted, he was sure. It was a war between artist and collector. If he could not win outright, at least he would not kiss the hem of her power with enthusiasm.

In the snow-dimmed studio, he sat in front of the easel and returned to work. After the detailed charcoal drawing on the canvas was complete, Deerfield began to fill in the spaces with washes of color thinned with turpentine. The painting took form—stonework in hues of raw sienna and trees behind with green blackness. It was a long view of the Cathedral entrance, looking east before sunrise, the front doors open. The silhouette of the mountains behind loomed ominous and uncivilized; the sky was a clear yellow-pink.

Tiers of candlesticks on the altar lit the rectangle of the interior to a deeper yellow than the sky. Was that amorphous shape someone praying at the altar? It was coming together, a painting that was more than a painting. Deerfield sensed an agreeable enduring quality in this work—it represented every cathedral and all cathedrals, and he knew that his art professors of years ago, who favored timelessness and universality, smiled over his shoulder as he painted.

Perhaps the gloomy light from a dark skylight was the very thing this painting needed. His hands now worked with resolve, mixing perfect colors and painting them on the canvas without hesitation. A swath of sunrise yellow from a wide brush fell right into place in the sky above the mountains, no correction needed. He inserted a thin red line down the right side of the building, curving over the elaborate cornices and moldings, and it brought the cathedral a little forward, like an island of foreign thought imposed, urban and dangerous, on this leafy New World setting. The painting was nearing completion.

Deerfield customarily put a finished painting face to the wall for a few weeks and then turned it around to search for clumsy passages. Because Mrs. Reilly wanted her painting delivered before Christmas, he would have to paint the final touches immediately.

He studied the work on the easel. It was a worthy piece, with strong, artistic touches: a long dribble of paint mixed too thin cascaded from the church door right to the canvas bottom. Deerfield relished that small accident, a testament to the very human hand of the painter. He preserved the drip through the Cathedral's steps, down across the forecourt and the evergreen plantings at the bottom of the canvas. In the mountain background of black-green conifers there were dangerous twists and circles, swirling Van Goghesque contortions in the highlands above the sleeping town. The painting suggested a war of ideas, incipient conflict, a quality that he sought to imbue in his work whenever the opportunity arose.

Then he had an idea. What if this was the very morning of a winter solstice long ago, when a band of Ancients was finishing a nightlong mountain ceremony? He would paint a fire in those hills above the Cathedral and a trail of smoke going heavenwards. Christianity front center, ancient ways behind. Even Mrs. Reilly's sharp eyes could not discern revolt in a simple bonfire.

Quickly mixing the colors, he painted a track of steel-gray threading upwards over the golden dawn, a smoky column rising to the top of the painting. He worked the colors on either side to mingle the smoke trail realistically into the sky. A small square of pure cadmium yellow in the circling darkness served as the bonfire. In his mind's eye, there were dancers in antlered headdresses and lines of shamans with peeled aspen staffs, painted bodies and acrid smoke in the square. He remembered these ceremonies from his pueblo childhood, when relatives sought to keep tradition alive among the often disinterested youngsters. It was a time when few elders dared to disbelieve, though the new generation yawned.

The telephone rang. It was Mrs. Reilly wanting her painting. Immediately.

Deerfield said, "It's not dry, Willa, so you'll have to keep it away from messy fingers."

"There are no such fingers at my house. It will be safe. The photographers are coming and we need your painting in its place. Bring a hammer and a nail, and don't forget your ladder."

The snow had stopped, so Deerfield slid the wet painting face up onto the bed of his pickup and drove carefully, deftly swerving around the many potholes and bumps between his studio and the Reilly mansion. After he hung his work above the silver-laden buffet table, heaped with platters of papier-mâché food, they both stood back to look.

"What do you think?" he asked. He knew it was good, so the question was only rhetorical.

"It works, David."

"That's all? It just works?"

"It's glorious, fabulous and you're a genius. Is that what you need? By the way, I love that small house in the background with its cheery fire. A mountain family waking early, no doubt, dressing for the first prayers in the Cathedral."

"You are a keen observer."

"I've added a little something to your check, my sweet. Merry Christ-mas." As he left, the magazine's photographers were adjusting the tall lights to illuminate her red and green buffet, a meal of painted turkeys and various plastic edibles for the center spread of an upcoming issue. The real buffet would be laid out several days later.

The check was for twice what he had asked. Why did he feel so unfulfilled? Small Spanish house or tribal bonfire, did it make a difference? That night he celebrated the Reilly munificence with artist friends, eating, drinking and laughing. That must have been the reason he slept so poorly, because he was wide awake before dawn.

It was a bit too early to have his usual breakfast of burrito and black coffee at the hotel dining room downtown. With the painting fresh in his mind, he parked just across the street from the darkened eatery, very near the imaginary point of view for his painting. It was a windless morning, just as in his picture, and he realized that it was also the exact day of the winter solstice.

The church's bronze doors were propped open to greet the early ar-rivals, that small circle who attend mass every morning. The golden interior beckoned the faithful and brought a guilty shudder to others. With a welling sense of pride, he understood that this actual view of the Cathedral was almost identical to his created scene. He could imagine his painted line of Chinese red slithering down the right side of the façade, suggesting some-thing aglow just out of the picture frame.

Then he looked up to the mountain behind and caught his breath. A bonfire sparkled through the trees, precisely where he had painted it, in the wilderness not available to day-hikers. Long filaments of smoke climbed slowly across the yellow sky, all but motionless. There was a happening high on the mountainside, a gathering there on this sacred day of people around a circle of high flames.

Was it a group of college students on a winter-break fantasy, athletic hikers out of their tents for a breakfast of dried eggs and bacon, talking by cell-phone to friends on the Gulf Coast? Or had the Old Ones returned for their long-awaited night, now celebrating this solstice dawn with a skin-wrapped, antlered dance, accompanied by thighbone flutes and taut drums? He could almost smell the secret herbs thrown with a flourish onto the fire in the last moments of the dance, the herbs that his Auntie collected for pueblo ceremonies. All the elders believed her mixture of dried native leaves and berries sent a supplication flying up to the stars. Since none of his cousins wanted to keep Auntie's Mason jars, they were still on a high shelf in his studio, slowly losing their potency.

David saw the fluorescent lights flickering and the waitress beckoned as she unlocked the door to the coffee shop. He walked across in the chilly air, his breath making trails behind him, the first customer of the day.

"No tortillas today for your burrito, David," she said. "Would you like a bowl of frijoles and soda crackers or some of yesterday's tamales?"

"I don't care, honey."

Deer Park

Witter Bynner's 1929 translation
of the Wang Wei poem

I could not help noticing how unmoved the widow was at the grave-side service, black veil never moving, her pale hands clasped together in front. Is that what veils are for, to hide the lack of sorrow, to conceal the truth from those who relish tears?

The minister's voice was deep-throated and woody, caressing the consonants and stretching out the vowels of the long-used words. *Forever and ever, life everlasting, world without end, Amen.* Our small gathering began the familiar hymn, singing hesitatingly in a mixture of keys as the coffin was lowered deeper and deeper. Surely by chance the concluding note sounded just as the wood struck bottom with a hollow thump. I wondered if any of the others saw the humor in that.

The strong aroma from the lilies atop the coffin was an odd extravagance, at the same time exotic and cloying in this simple ceremony for such a respected man, a longtime friend. The scent grew stronger and stronger, then dissipated when the dirt was shoveled in. I took her hand in mine as we walked back to the line of black cars, parked close together, with drivers in uniform, caps in hand, paid well to look sad.

"Let's walk, instead," she said.

"It's not far, back to the house," I said.

"No, I know another place."

Without us, her driver drove away directly behind the emptied hearse, the other mourners' cars following back towards the town, like black beetles in a primordial procession. The sound of the engines diminished, too, until it was silent, with only some faraway finches adding afternoon grace notes.

The cemetery was on a hill, the first step up to the wooded mountains from the town below. It was easy for us to walk slowly towards the trees among the other gravesites and headstones, where dead patriarchs lay beneath granite obelisks and flu-taken children slept under small marble lambs. We passed through an iron gate with speared spindles to the grove of beech trees that adjoined. Their elephant-gray trunks went straight into the ground, not splaying out like those of the lesser trees which were uncherished for quarter-sawn flooring and rolling pins. Under the beeches lay nothing else—no seedling trees or grasses—but a moist, deep mat of fallen leaves that muffled our steps. She, still veiled, led me through the succession of wrinkled trunks to where the fir trees began.

"This is my favorite part, where the black trunks are. Do you like their darkness?" she asked.

"I do, but watch your step, the path is getting narrower," I said.

"I shall. Nobody else comes this far."

But I thought I heard voices behind us, as if a group were following in our footsteps, keeping a respectful distance from the new widow. They were not angry voices, but many together, talking over each other. When I turned my head to listen, the voices stopped as if we were being spied upon. Were the woods ahead of us empty of these voices?

Deeper we went, twisting our bodies in the narrow places to keep our hands clasped, not to lose the link. The matted leaves turned into moldering pine needles as the trees grew closer together. With brisker steps we carried on in wordless anticipation. The western sun broke through to light an opening in the trees, a meadow, as we walked into it. The low light made our shadows long and thin.

We lay close to each other on the soft grasses in the last of the sunlight. I still kept an ear out for the voices that had been following us, lest they come upon us and discover our secret. She did not seem to care, her head resting on the now neatly folded veil, but I knew the eyes of woods-hidden deer watched us, wondering what was going on in their forest.

Afterwards, after our love, the only sunlight that remained was high up on the green moss where the last ray cut through the dark trunks. We stayed there for a while, looking up, until the edge of darkness came.

"It's time to go back, I guess," I said.

"I know the way, even in the dark. Take my hand, my dear."

Leaving the empty mountain woods, we retraced our steps through the fir trees, past where I thought I heard the voices, across the grove of beeches with the ankle-deep leaves, outside the cemetery with its cast-iron fencing and down towards the town. As the gravel road turned into a curbed street with two-story houses, yellow lights in their windows, she turned and kissed me. Our separate lives awaited, loved ones wondering where we had gone and what to do with our cold suppers.

Beethoven's Slippers

*A monodrama libretto
for a full-bodied woman's voice,
speaking and singing with
an accompanying string quartet.*

Charles gave me the slippers.
See them over on the piano,
tattered but still there on their stand.
We ran off to Paris after the war,
taking a flat on Rue de Bac. Mother, thinking
I had secretly married upstate,
paid for the entire trip, seven months away from
my innocent sisters and everyone else in Mount
Pleasant. First class, portside staterooms,
caviar on toast points every night at sea.
The boulevards were shiny gray when we arrived.
In the beginning, it was bliss,
dinners at the bistro downstairs,
much red wine, falling into bed
after midnight. Charles was so handsome,
with his dark hair and sad umber eyes.

Love came in the morning,
when everything worked so well. Afterwards,
we walked for hours on the nearby streets.
        There was a musical curiosities shop
in Rue des Saints Pères. A lighted window
with green mullions. We looked in,
umbrellas up. Day after day, something new.
        From the last century a famous baton,
inlaid with ivory and obsidian stripes.
A conductor's grandson needed train fare to the south.
        Manuscript pages five through nine,
yellow parchment with spots, an easy etude for four
hands, composer unknown. Brahms suspected.
Six thousand for them all.
        Opera glasses from Milan with tortoise-shell insets,
assured to be Verdi's own. Ten thousand francs in blue ink.
        And one fine day, there they were
on a stand with cabriole legs.
The Original Slippers of Beethoven,
the sign said, of doeskin from the Black Forest,
embroidered in scarlet silk by Lutheran nuns.
Across the toes was a view of Bonn, half the town
on each foot. Provenance guaranteed.
Twenty thousand francs in brown ink.
        I love those, I told Charles
with my best smile. I will keep them
on the Chickering back home.
Even Mother should approve.
Sisters Emma Lou and Adelaide,
still unmarried, will envy my improving
arpeggios. Sensibly, Charles said
to wait until Mother's next check arrived.

But that was a ruse. The very next day
he traded his father's gold watch, a Girard-Perregaux,
which chimed the quarter hour and predicted
the dark of moon, for the slippers.
A secret bit of business, between his errands.

      At the bistro that night,
when I did not hear the soft chimes
beneath his English tweeds, he confessed.
The great man's slippers were mine forever.
We drank a toast and I was so happy.

      Naughty me wore them
around the apartment, waltzing on the parquet
when Charles was not there. Beethoven had
very small feet for such large music.

      After several months, it was easier to let
Charles pay the bills on his own. Mother's
money was his as much as mine.
The days grew longer and Charles gave me a
string of China pearls on check day.

      Then a pair of diamond clips in the shape
of sailing ships, each different, and a month later,
a pale Fortuny frock with a hundred pleats, buttons of lapis.

      Like a country girl, I wore them together
on Bastille Day—pearls, pleats, and clips. We laughed
until it hurt as fireworks flamed above the Seine.
We sailed home that fall.

      I remember Charles mostly for the slippers now.
Mother disliked him and the mention of his name
made my Father, the banker, sneeze. That mountebank
is not welcome at our house, he said.
There was a chemical something between them, I think.

      Charles and I drove West in my two-seater,

to this town of art and music, painters, writers and composers
on every street, studios alight until dawn.
People dressed however they liked: rouge circles on cheeks,
headbands with coral beads and long dresses at any hour.

        We met the whole town: the archbishop, the mayor,
the famous aviatrix, the buxom saloonkeeper,
and a tall woman painter with a small head.
Charles had trouble with their names and
could not recall their faces. The town had strange curves
and sudden angles, lanes with no outlet.
He missed the classic order of the East Coast,
its streets clearly marked.

        We fell out of love slowly in the small house
along the park—like water leaking from a bowl
with a thin crack, the bouquet withering in stages.

        He left the next summer, in my two-seater.
My parting gift, the car and a kiss. I heard that
he married a sweet-corn heiress from Des Moines,
I supposed with harsh blonde curls and Prussian ankles
from standing at the stove.

        Charles and I were never actually married,
although I had told everybody so.
In Paris nobody cared. Or here, for that matter,
where art, song, and poetry were always in the air.

        My parents are gone, thirty years now in the Franklin
Street cemetery. We three sisters sold the house
and ordered up a granite obelisk with doves on the wing.
Lady Banks climbs around it every spring, her yellow roses
covering the shiny black.

        I do not have the pearls or the diamond clips
anymore, but the slippers are atop the piano
on their stand, impressively crumpled. There is

more shade at the house now. The piñons press up
against the windowpanes, and I can barely see across the park.
I may need a new roof before snow.

      On sixteen December, I had my friends
over to celebrate Ludwig's birthday again. There was a young
poetess with promise, a thin lad who carves wooden festoons,
a printmaker with well-behaved Afghans and another, younger
woman painter with a small head. French wine and the caviar
toast points, full moon shining over the snow-covered park.

      With all seated and talk stopped,
I played the Sonata, wearing the Fortuny pleats and the
slippers once again. I raised my hands high at the end
to a small rain of applause. Not too bad for a Mount Pleasant girl.

      The slippers have become scruffy,
their red silk unraveling. I sent Charles and
his farmland heiress a snapshot of the soiree,
the fresh-faced crowd surrounding me
with raised glasses of white burgundy, forefingers
pointing down to my slippers. It was so gay.

      People said the evening was magic,
but Charles never wrote back.

Mummy Brown

One of the favorite colors of the Pre-Raphaelite painters was called Mummy Brown—and not out of joking affection. It was a warm pigment made from the bitumen used by ancient Egyptians to embalm their dead, famed for its preservative powers.

But now even Mummy Brown is gone altogether. Geoffrey Roberson-Park, managing director of London's venerable C. Roberson Color Makers, regretfully admits that the firm has run out of mummies. "We might have a few odd limbs lying around somewhere," he apologized, "but not enough to make any more paint. We sold our last complete mummy some years ago for, I think £3. Perhaps we shouldn't have. We certainly can't get any more."

—*Time Magazine*, Oct 2, 1964

Patty Ann and Gerald Boxwood were having breakfast outdoors at the table against the east-facing wall, maybe the last meal of the season before frost and snow made this daily indulgence impossible. The cheese omelet they shared was finished, as were the toast and sausages, so they were savoring the last of the coffee in the warm sun. She read the local paper and he the new issue of Time, relishing stories of happenings on the East Coast and the world beyond.

"Look here," he said, "no more Mummy Brown. London painters must be in an uproar."

"Why ever?"

"They ran out of full length mummies. Only a few legs or arms are left."

"I still have a whole tube on my table, I'm sure."

"Should we buy you a lot more from the art supply before they're all gone?"

"I've heard that Vandyke Brown is just the same."

She rattled the paper for emphasis and folded it down to a quarter segment, the way everyone did in the city. Her mind went back to local events, city council meetings and obituaries, never imagining what a great change might be coming their way because of Gerald's news. In many ways, Vandyke Brown was not the same as Mummy, but time would have to make that known to the couple.

Patty Ann was a painter whose realistic paintings of traditional flower arrangements had supported the couple for almost two decades, a necessity since Gerald's poems produced a small adoring audience but little income. Theirs was nonetheless a marriage of equals, because Gerald, while turning out his yearly poem or two, looked after the house, pruned back the garden, cooked the meals, paid the bills and did everything else to give Patty Ann undisturbed hours in the studio. Neither was annoyed by this division of tasks, but instead both felt fortunate to be part of a talented twosome, noted by their friends for reciprocal love and respect. She was tall and thin, he a broad-shouldered but bookish country boy. In many ways, except for not producing children, theirs was a perfect marriage, as each did what the other could not or did not want to do.

They had met in New York in the last years of the Second World War, when she was a third-year student at The Art Students League, and he was working as a first reader for Little, Brown. His slight limp had not allowed him to serve in the army. After her graduation, their courtship and wedding, Gerald received a small inheritance from his grandmother, which more than allowed them to leave the city and drive to Santa Fe to follow their individual paths.

Gerald's passion was the sonnet, which he could rework and polish for long hours. Hers was to emulate the Dutch floral paintings of the seventeenth century, to use their classical secrets to illuminate her own modern and unique canvases. Right from the start of their time together, they knew their roles with regard to each other's work: she read his poems with only light comment, he made encouraging remarks about her flowers.

With Grandmother Boxwood's money they bought a simple house on Santa Fe's north side that had a view of both the Sangre de Cristo Mountains and the city lights below. There was a large room in the rear of the house for Patty Ann's studio and three others for ordinary use. They felt they could survive on the money left over for three or four years, if they were frugal.

Gerald immediately planted a flower garden, raising most of the perennials from seed or buying small pots at garden club benefits. It was important for Patty Ann to have access to real flowers for her work, for her bouquets. In between household and garden tasks, Gerald labored over his sonnets, each of them taking many months. It would be ten years before he completed his first book, which was published by the house he used to work for in New York in a buckram edition of five hundred copies. By then every penny of Grandmother's bequest had been consumed, so they lived almost solely on the proceeds of Patty Ann's bouquets. Gerald's handsome volume, poems of new beginnings and hope, brought in only the occasional small royalty check.

Patty Ann's paintings took almost as long as did Gerald's first poem. Each flower was drawn separately after coming into bloom in his garden border. She was not interested in representing all the flowers at the actual week of their blooming, but like the Dutch masters included spring tulips with autumn chrysanthemums, as well as lilies and delphinium from the months between. One blossom might require a whole day of work, or two or three if it had a complex umbel.

The couple created their art in the same painstaking way. Gerald used words like jewels, inserting them with care, repositioning them again and again as new ideas occurred, then buffing the result to a lapidary sparkle. Patty Ann's individual blossoms took thirty or more coverings, as she shaded the curving stems and leaves from light to dark, yellow to green, green to black. She glazed a single flower petal in a similar manner, enriching the colors to a porcelain finish. The white base pushed up through the clear strata, resulting in an opalescent quality not possible to achieve with solid paints.

She learned to glaze the background with layer after layer of transparent Mummy in a thick linseed oil mixture over a white ground. The individual blooms fairly popped out of this rich dark soup, making it worth the time it took for each layer to fully dry before the next was applied.

In their second year in Santa Fe, a downtown gallery owner, Devon McNair, heard about Patty Ann's work at the horticultural society meeting where both he and Gerald were members. At the society meeting's close, he asked Gerald if he could follow him home for a visit to her studio. This was a time when galleries actually purchased paintings before reselling them to collectors, and McNair made out a check for Patty Ann's first three panels that same day. The paintings sold within the week to his most prized customer, a collector with a large, historic house and a hunger for new paintings.

McNair let the paintings go for a great deal more money than he paid Patty Ann, so he was very pleased with his purchase. Other gallery owners said McNair's high regard for profit was matched only by his perfect eye, the exact qualities needed to make his Santa Fe's most successful gallery.

It was now 1964 and Patty Ann's paintings brought substantially more each time they changed hands. McNair had lessened the gap between what he and she pocketed from her art, and life was good at the Boxwood house. The pattern of the couple's days was set: breakfast together, then all day working apart until evening. Gerald would clean up the breakfast table, as he always did. She noted the clock on the wall of her studio, nine-thirty, and knew that if she could work five or six good hours each day, a new picture would be finished each month or so.

It was best to get right at it, painting the first stroke the minute she sat down. Then the cadence of the day would take over. She squeezed a short line of Mummy Brown oil paint onto her palette, admiring its rich yellowish brown, dark with a touch of Chinese red, like deep amber. Mixed with passages of burnt umber and ultramarine, it constituted the deep wall color behind her floral paintings. Collectors remarked on her striking use of light, but she knew that it was the Mummy in the background that set off everything painted in front of it. She had read that Rembrandt and Vermeer before her had used the exact same paint for their backgrounds and felt a secret connection with them, despite the separating centuries. Could a smidgen of one Egyptian nobleman be mingled into each of their paintings?

Patty Ann did not paint on canvas. She prepared her own painting blocks, quarter-sawn slabs of red oak, with layers of gesso, sanding each coat lightly with rottenstone papers from a shop in Florence. Running her hand like a reader of Braille over the surface with her eyes shut, she judged the smoothness by touch alone. A single panel could take several weeks of her afternoon, away-from-the-easel hours. The slightest flaw or bump must be corrected.

The current painting on her easel was a classic tabletop composition, the vase in the middle of a round table covered in the folds of a patterned scarf. In her mind, it would include only white flowers, shaded from the deepest ivory lilies to the intense, laundry white of Shasta daisies. She thought that the varied colors in the typical Dutch floral paintings were too undisciplined, too obvious. Her best work was often a monochromatic bouquet, all red flowers or all yellows, hinting to the cognoscenti that this was a modern painting, not merely a deft copy.

She toured Gerald's flower borders with regularity, noticing which plants were coming into full bloom. With a sixth sense of her wishes, Gerald from time to time delivered the new blossom, often without discussion. Her bouquet grew a stem at a time, each flower going where it was intended in the conceptual design. Between the flowers she included grasses and leaves of many patterns, the fullness increasing each day.

When the flowers were finished, the background of Mummy would begin. It could take an entire week to paint the rich brown background between all the petals and leaves. She mixed each brush load separately so that the wall appeared to shimmer almost imperceptibly with different shades of the brown. As the layers built up, the flowers fairly jumped forward. She found places for small insects and thin white lines along the edges of the petals.

After Patty Ann had completed a dozen more paintings, her tube of Mummy was empty. The art supplier on Canyon Road said that Mummy was, indeed, forever unavailable, so she replaced it with a full tube of the best English Vandyke brown. She remembered Gerald's suggestion to buy a lifetime supply of Mummy and wondered why she had not.

The troubles started immediately. Vandyke did not have the transparent tortoise-shell quality so important to her backgrounds. Even Gerald noticed a muddiness, a certain opacity in the wall behind the flowers in her new piece, but he kept an uxorious silence. She, of course, saw this as well but plugged along, finishing the new work entirely with the Vandyke. Who would have thought how different it was from the Mummy? The Artist's Handbook listed them as being identical colors, although the Vandyke was said to suffer fewer fugitive problems and therefore to be preferred.

When she delivered the new picture to the gallery McNair was not as charitable as Gerald had been. He said, "The flowers are beautiful, Patty Ann, but this new work doesn't have your usual luster. Have you been in a bad mood?"

"Nothing's different, Devon."

"But there is something different. I can't quite put my finger on it. The wall, I think."

He stood back with his hands on his hips and studied the new piece. Then he picked it up in his hands and held it at arm's length. What did this change portend? Would all the new Boxwood paintings have this hidden, annoying lack of spirit? Had his cash cow run dry?

She said, "I'll try a moleskin background for the next one, Devon.

I've read that Marie Antoinette loved it and had the paneling of her personal salons washed in moleskin—lovely, rich gray that makes pale yellow just sing."

"Doesn't sound promising—moleskin. Maybe we can think of a different word for it when I do my presentations. Oyster shell or thundercloud. Certainly not the name of a headless queen."

And the collectors noticed something, as well. Whereas earlier paintings had left the gallery in a day or two, this new one remained unsold for weeks. McNair reluctantly moved it to a side wall, as its former window position was too valuable to waste on a flawed work. Several months went by before a customer from out of town bought the new opaque-walled piece, but only after McNair offered him a deep discount.

Matters slowly grew worse. As collectors avoided her current work, Patty Ann's confidence, formerly as strong as a rising rocket, was shaken. She noticed a tremble in her hand as she started a new piece and she grew unsure of foreground colors as well. Perhaps it was just a phase, she thought, gone through by many artists she had read about. Losing Mummy on her palette was like losing a good friend, and the grieving must end in time. Matisse once did not paint for a year, and Picasso destroyed a pile of questionable work. Things would get better later on.

However, it finally became obvious to both herself and Gerald that things were not going to get better. Patrons at the McNair Gallery asked for "Early Boxwoods" now, and her current work was shown in the low-ceilinged, airless back room. McNair himself was solicitous and kind to Patty Ann, but his attention moved on to newer, younger members of his roster.

Hope was renewed for a brief spell when Gerald found a box of small tubes of Mummy, a Turkish brand, at the estate sale of an old Santa Fe landscapist. But when Patty Ann tried to use one of them, the paint separated into an oily ochre and hard nuggets of a blackish-brown, no doubt the mummy returning to its basic parts.

Patty Ann's new paintings stopped selling altogether, and McNair switched from his policy of outright purchase to one of consignment, eliminating all risk to him. Rather than face the sympathetic looks of the staff at the McNair Gallery, Patty Ann began to let her panels build up in stacks against her studio wall. Because of this dispiritedness, her production slowed to a mere two paintings a year—the rocket of all possibilities had come to ground.

In the odd symmetry between two who live together, Gerald's new collection of sonnets earned high acclaim from popular critics and academics. All of these poems were about decline and fall. Not since Edna St. Vincent Millay had a book of poetry sold so well, and translated editions for Europe were well under way, publishers there vying for a chance at them. Little, Brown sent a handsome advance for all of Gerald's future writing, which galvanized him into longer hours at the writing desk.

With the same intensity she had given her paintings, Patty Ann became a better cook than Gerald ever was, mastering French sauces and handmade Italian pastas. As her studio grew dusty, the kitchen overflowed with activity. The most difficult, protracted recipe only increased her resolve to master it, even if this meant special ordering of mandolin slicers or copper bains-marie. Guests coming to their popular house for her excellent dinners learned to walk with rapid steps, looking neither left nor right, through the flower borders previously so well-tended by Gerald, now reduced to drifts of brown iris encircled with crabgrass, and small clumps of leaves where daffodils once bloomed. The aroma of a pork roast braised in milk wafted through the open door.

Nirvana

On my way to the California coast, I was staying overnight in Palm Springs, a houseguest of my friend Bob Fortunna. We were on time for the reservation at Davey's, as Bob claimed that the owners relished giving away the tables of late arrivals. The main room, almost full with middle-aged and older men, some accompanied by buffed, younger companions, was encircled with booths, larger tables spread across the center. The room was noisy with conversation. The owner seated us at the one remaining empty booth, which was furnished with green leather cushions and overhung by a low lamp in the shape of an inverted magnolia blossom.

After we had ordered medium-rare steaks with no potatoes and green salads with dressing on the side, Bob said, "Excuse me for a moment. I see some dear friends that I have to talk to." He walked over to a far booth and stood talking to a white-haired and balding foursome.

The room was full of men enjoying their own kind. How comfortable Palm Springs was—gay bars, gay restaurants and entire gay neighborhoods. For a small city, it was a haven of tolerance. I thought of Eleanor, my old Santa Fe neighbor and a shopkeeper, who was convinced that summer Bible students from Glorieta, ignoring one of their great commandments, shoplift-ed small items from her store. She put a sign on the screen door: *No Baptists*. Palm Springs did not need to erect a *No Bigots* sign, because the judgmental knew better than to tarry here.

As I was looking around the room, a wide-shouldered man with a small waist, certainly a body-builder, came up to the table and said, "You are beautiful." His smile revealed perfect teeth.

Caught by total surprise, I pulled enough wits together to say, "Sit down, let's talk."

He moved into the seat opposite me with cat-like ease. His face was broad and square, his hair cut short like a military man's.

"Is that your lover over there?" he asked. His basso voice was as deep as Mozart's silver-haired Commenditore.

"No, a good friend. I'm staying tonight in his guest room. A one-night visit."

"He's a lucky man."

I thought with amusement of this reversal. I was customarily the one who walked up to the table of a younger man, charming him, inviting him. In this paradise for older men, I was the prey and experienced the warm, new feeling of being wanted.

"Do you live in Palm Springs?" I asked.

"Four years now."

"Life seems good here."

"It is. Can you come home with me after dinner, without your good friend?"

"No, thanks, I can't. What part of town do you live in?"

"Nirvana for you, but most people call it Deep Well Ranch."

"Where did you pick up such a persuasive way of talking?"

"It comes naturally when I want something. Why don't you stay a while longer? If only for a few days. I will make love to you and we can get acquainted."

He reached across the pool of light and put his two hands over mine. They were warm, tanned, and curiously smooth for being so large. It was an agreeable change to be touched in anticipation of something more, and I felt a small electrical charge that I missed in everyday contact. I wondered if I should accept his offer.

"I'm going to Glitter Bay for a working summer, to finish my novel," I said. "I'll be back through in September."

"Here's my card, Mr. Glitter Bay. My name's Axton. Call when you come here again. You can slowly read to me what you've written, while I stroke your chest, fondle your brow, make you crazy with desire."

"How could I say no?" As he stood up to leave, he leaned down, put a hand behind my head and firmly pulled me into his kiss. It was short and he tasted slightly of Martini; afterwards, he smiled directly at me.

Bob, as well as the four men he had gone across the room to meet, all turned their heads my way as Axton returned to his own booth behind me. If Palm Springs was the fabled sophisticated retreat from Los Angeles, a spirited curiosity lived here as much as in any small town. I gave a thumbs-up to the group. What would Axton have said if I had replied that Bob was my lover? Much the same, I thought.

Bob returned and sat down. "It didn't take you long to feel right at home. My friends were impressed."

"I didn't summon him, he just came over. Do you know him? His name is Axton."

"We see him at the gym, but he never gave us a welcome like that. They say that he was an Air Force colonel, a jet bomber pilot and a marine sergeant before that. He lives well on a double military pension. Double-chromosomes, too, from the look of it."

So he was really Don Giovanni's father-in-law, winged helmet and all, perhaps just now exploring a nature kept under wraps during two successive enlistments. For a moment, I thought it unkind of me to put him off, but all things would be possible on my return, after the completion of my novel. It was like money in the bank, the interest compounding by the day.

"Bob, I'm not really on the market," I said.

"Nonsense. We're always on the market. It's what we are."

That night as I turned out the light in Bob's guest room, nestled down in the air-conditioned comfort, it felt good to be noticed again, to be sought out. My sensual part having been for so long turned down low, I could now feel the first bubbles of steam coursing up from below. How different California was from my small town. People here said right away what they wanted, making overt advances with the first breath. I had become accus-tomed to the reticence among my circle of friends at home. Where would this tearing down of fences lead? Did a new life await me on the California coast?

Do Something for Her

Our community of artists came together years ago at the end of Camino Militar, where parcels of land cost a tenth as much as the lots on smarter streets. Tracts carved out of corrals and ramshackle farms were good enough for artists, people said. Bohemians were tasteless, lazy, and poor, so it was better if they stayed out on the edge of Santa Fe.

This bargain land afforded us immediate access to the mountain wilderness, but had no important views. After clearing away the goat pens and rusted car bodies, we helped each other put up our houses and studios, carting loads of adobe bricks along the dirt road, laying them up, raising the beams and learning to plaster the rough walls. I had a way with designing floor plans and offered my services free to the others. Even if no prizes were awarded, the resultant neighborhood had its wayward charm and I was considered the architectural guru of the group.

As can happen with real estate matters, the Militar properties came to be greatly prized and were seldom on the market. Prices tripled, then tri-pled again, and several of my neighbors sold out, buying with the proceeds waterfront places in the Caribbean or more acreage farther out from town. I remained steadfast, however, in rejecting all offers and instructed my execu-tor to dispose of my property when the time came. I planned to leave Militar in the Packard hearse, the one with cut-glass windows that I on occasion saw parked near the Cathedral. My next door neighbor, Alicia Rutherford, another holdout, promised to deliver her best rendition of *Panis Angelicus* at my funeral service in her reedy, high-register voice. I did not expect to die soon, despite the infrequent episodes of blurred vision.

My studio grew over the years, as I added onto the original structure a book-shelved office, then a tall room with floor space for several easels. It was a handsome and comfortable space in which to paint, with light from the skylights and the mountain-view windows mingling into a warm, clear white. That light diminished in winter and my paintings from those months always became more introspective.

The latest addition to my eight acres was a temple, small by ancient standards, but correctly proportioned and perfectly sited with the columned portico facing south. It took me most of a year to build, with the help of a varying crew of helpers. The stonework was coarser than you might see along the Aegean, although it was without question Hellenic. Sometimes a bit unsteady on the high ladder, I carved the embellishments myself, with a hammer and chisel I had not used since art school. In many ways, the temple changed my life.

But I am getting ahead of my story, which began last July on the Greek island of Tinos. Richard and I were there for the month, our rented house unseen until we arrived late on a hot afternoon. The ferry from Athens deposited us on the quay, each of us with a rucksack and duffle bag. It was to be our month away from the world; we would read, swim, and unwind. Tinos was a quiet island favored less by tourists than by devout pilgrims, scores of whom each weekend clambered up to its basilica on their knees. The disco-and-nude-beach set continued on with the ferry for the half-hour trip to Mykonos.

Our house on Tinos was disappointing, crowded among three others in a small village compound. From the upper floor, the bedroom balcony afforded a view across rooftops to the horizon. If I stretched, I could see a sliver of the promised sea view above the red tiles and satellite dishes. I wondered if we had come to the wrong island, but our month's rent was nonrefundable.

The days fell into a pattern: breakfast at the *taverna* beside the harbor, a swim from the beach around the bend, and several midday hours in a rented Jeep exploring the island. Afternoons I worked on my sketchbook, refining my ideas for a series of Cycladic village paintings. Richard continued his lifelong spiritual journal, clicking away each day on a laptop. Sometimes we took an afternoon swim at another beach. We had our suppers late, as there was little else to do after sunset on Tinos. We were asleep by eleven, imagining we could hear across the water the night music from Mykonos.

In the third week of our stay we discovered a village on the east slope of the island, the last on the peripheral road. The Jeep had proven worthy and on this day Richard braked to a sudden stop as the road played out against a short curving wall. A spring gurgled from its opposite side and coursed down through a small sloping village to the sea. Nothing was shown on my map, but there they were, fifty or so whitewashed houses, embraced by dark cypresses.

Richard took out the Jeep's keys and we walked down the rough stone staircase next to the running water. Houses on either side of the stream crowded in to make a narrow lane, with the sound of dripping water echoing against the masonry walls. The houses were closed and shuttered until midway down, where we spotted an open door. An old woman sat just inside, breaking string beans into a bowl on her black lap. She did not look up from her beans. As she made no response to my simple *kalimera*, I suspected her to be deaf.

Richard and I continued down the pathway, which alternated between narrow ramps and uneven steps. After passing through the stone-basined washhouse at the bottom of the village, the stream coursed under the perimeter wall to irrigate a grove of old pears and stunted apple trees overrun with vines. We sat on the stone bench in the washhouse and considered what we had just seen.

"Who needs more?" Richard asked. "Houses away from the world, water, an orchard and these stone basins to wash our clothes."

"To me it seems lonely," I replied. "All the houses are shut tight. How can we meet the neighbors, gossip or borrow some ouzo?"

He was not listening. "We could buy a place here. Spend part of the year, and I would go on to my lessons in India. You could stay and sketch."

"What fun, having cocktails each night with the string-bean lady after you've left!"

"And I'm sure life is healthier here in the Aegean breezes. Your migraines and troubles breathing might just vanish forever."

"Doctor Miller would be delighted to be rid of me."

"There's a real estate office near our breakfast taverna. They will know about this village, what's for sale."

The woman was not to be seen when we climbed back up, her door shut. Looking more closely at the spring by the road, we made out the remnants of a marble surround, engaged columns with weathered striations and a stained arch above the water pipe. Dense trunks of ivy and an old yew tree almost hid the source.

Richard pointed to the marble edging and said, "There were shrines to the goddess on every Greek island. This could be much older than it looks."

The idea that we had perhaps discovered an ancient site, forgotten by the locals, excited us both for the rest of the trip. However, the real estate agent in Tinos discouraged us from looking for property in that village. Nothing there had changed hands in his lifetime, he said. It would do no good to knock on doors and enquire on our own. Foreigners were not welcome. The month came to a close without our returning to the spring-washed village, but we talked about it every day.

On the twelve-hour return flight from Athens to New York, I slept for a fitful few hours. Daylight and the farewell dinner's *retsina* fought against my natural inclination for easy sleep. I dreamt about the village—the old woman, now chatty, grew in height and showed us rooms scented with odd spices and musk, the shutters opened to the sea beyond. When I described my dream to Richard, who seldom slept on planes, he was sure it represented a positive, encouraging omen. We must continue the hunt on Tinos, he said, where we might find our home in the very beating heart of Greek mysticism.

Maybe the old woman was the goddess in modern dress. Now she smiled, a rare gift in any century. How lucky I was to have a dream like that, he said.

I myself do not believe in prophetic signs, but back at home Richard had always seen them everywhere, every day. They were birds that tarried in our garden, double rainbows, a door slamming with force in a slight breeze, books that fell off tables, a resident squirrel staring too fervently into the lower panes of the French doors or an egg rolling itself off the counter. Each held its own message. He said that we would regret it if we did not follow my dream's portent.

After a week at home in the house on Militar, Richard was packing for his next trip to the Himalayan foothills. He was heading to a famous cave, one of a group converted into quarters for meditation. Having paid ten months' rent in advance, he planned to follow the classic *Ngondro*, with its million prostrations and its diet of rice and dal. Truth and beauty would surely ensue. I suspected that instead of achieving enlightenment, he would soon develop back pain, attract spider bites and suffer chronic indigestion, and as in the past, lose a great deal of weight, returning home with a serious cough.

"I'll miss you, Richard."

"You'll be fine."

I was not so sure. "It won't be the same here when you're gone. I can't iron a collar like you can or fry the eggs without that brown lace."

"Why don't you stay busy with a building project? You love to build."

"I do, but the house and studio are finished."

"What about a stone temple?"

"For Buddha?" I did not share his fascination.

"No, the middle path is just right for me. I see the old goddess as yours, like needy women the world over."

"You can be a prick, Richard. A temple. Where?"

"Next to the spring at the far back. It runs for a few months every year. She likes evergreens and running water."

"It is a nice spring."

As he rolled up a brass bell in his year's supply of white blessing scarves, he said, "Do something for the goddess, and she'll do something for you. We've forgotten that simple formula in the modern West. And remember to plant the ivy and the yew around it, like on the island."

"I'll think about it."

"Ramiro and Victor can help you before they go back to Mexico for the winter. They're good with stone." The Tibetan prayer cards exactly fit inside his leather sandals, completing his packing.

"Maybe later. I'm out of cash now."

"Well, Alicia is always next door to keep you company."

Sad at his departure, I drove us downtown to meet the shuttle-bus to the airport. Richard was cheery, however, as he gathered up his rucksack and waved to me from the van window. He had gained back the lost weight from the last trip to India, and his dark hair was restored to shiny health. Now he was returning to that land of fevers and worms. What is so compelling about an insect-infested prayer cave, anyway? I know. Buddha. I thought he must see my bittersweet smile as I waved back.

Alicia sensed my melancholy and that night asked me to dinner. We talked about Richard's departure and his building suggestion. Alicia thought it a splendid idea for me to build a temple to the prehistoric goddess right in her own neighborhood. She could bring offerings of rice cakes and wild flowers on her morning walks, asking only for small favors, woman to woman.

"It will cost a lot," I said. "I'm broke right now."

"That can change," she said.

"I don't relish holding a fund-raiser for it. *Local Painter Seeks Your Spiritual Donations.* I'll just wait for the omen, as Richard says."

"So what would that be?"

"A chunk of money. If the goddess wants her temple, she can stand up and part the seas a little, make things happen."

In the weeks that followed, I worked at being on my own again. I upped my morning painting schedule to include afternoons as well. The

Cycladic village paintings began to fall into place. I found time for a daily walk with Alicia and thought about changing my diet. The temple stayed in my mind like a familiar melody, playing itself again and again.

Several times at sunset, I walked to the far back of the property to watch the spring burble. There was a slight rise in the ground there, the land beyond turning into a forested backdrop of ponderosa pines and junipers. I wondered who chose the sites for the ancient temples. Did a favored priest, full of himself and his high position, stroll the pristine woods looking for the exact confluence of a water source, an eminence of ground and a view to the horizon? I needed no such expert. Richard was right, this was the spot.

Another piece of the puzzle dropped into place when my gallery director called to report the sale of four of my Greek village paintings. A new woman collector, he said, tall and bold, walked in from the street, paid in cash (so unusual nowadays) and asked for the canvases to be shipped to a warehouse in Europe.

It was a sum large enough to cover my winter living expenses and to give me a start on building the temple. I asked Victor and Ramiro to begin that very day. In a downtown bookshop Alicia had found a leather-bound volume of lithographs from an Englishwoman's grand tour—pyramids, Roman arches, Mediterranean waterfronts, Moroccan street scenes and, there it was, a small pagan temple from the Anatolian coast. In the margins someone had sketched the floor plan in brown ink as well as details of the carving on the pediment. I scaled my temple to match and found every piece needed for its completion almost by magic at the precise time that it was needed.

I found four black granite columns online. They were in the stone yards of a Tennessee man who had collected architectural remnants as a sideline to his headstone business. His new wife wanted him to downsize, empty the yard and take her on cruises. He asked no shipping charge, glad to be rid of the old things. The slate roof-tiles came from a house being torn down for our city hall expansion. My very last purchase was a goat-footed tripod from an estate sale, designed as a bronze incense dish but serving instead as a comfortable home for someone's beloved fern.

By the beginning of the next summer the temple and its paved fore-court were finished, waiting for the pilgrims and their adorations. I planted plugs of creeping thyme between the flagstones to give off an herbal fragrance when visitors walked upon them. I paid the last bills after selling two more paintings to another collector.

Alicia came to admire the finished temple, now her project as much as mine. I had designed benches for each side of the forecourt for the weary devout and for us infidels, with wine, at the end of the day. Seedling yews lined the walkway and the young ivy plants put out clambering new tendrils. As a flock of martins circled above us, I thought I could smell the salt-water spray of the Aegean and an exotic new smell, perhaps a Turkish incense.

"We need some sort of ceremony," Alicia said.

"I doubt we'll find a pagan priest, even in Santa Fe."

"I don't know. My friend Beata Kinsworth, the archaeologist, is almost one. She has degrees from Cambridge and knows everything about the classical world. She re-reads the ten volumes of Herodotus from front to back every year."

"Can you ask her to come by and tell us what is appropriate? Exciting, isn't it, like firing up a furnace for the first winter?"

Dr. Kinsworth would meet us the next afternoon. I was waiting at the temple when she arrived with Alicia. Kinsworth was a short woman with steely grey hair in tight curls, and the wrinkled face that comes from years in the New Mexico sun. She walked forcefully, but with a slight limp, one long step, one short, her cane swinging up between steps. I imagined Alicia as a willowy duchess taking her lame bulldog on a country outing—patrician height accompanied by pugnacious solidity. Kinsworth brushed aside my greeting to point her cane up to the temple's frieze, which I had carved with such pains.

She said, "Bad business there on the pediment, but, at first glance, an honest replica. Unsophisticated more than crude. Artemis would be tolerant, I think, and pleased."

I watched as she inspected the rest of the building, running her hand along the stonework. She picked at the mortar, moved in for a closer look and leaned over to study the stone-circled spring, which had been especially fulsome in these last months. Rapping a wordless approval with her stick on a black column, she moved slowly inside to bend over the bronze dish, sniffing. The coffers of the temple ceiling brought a short frown to her face but no outright disdain. She closed in on one of the side niches, looking up into its corners. I wondered if an architect in ancient Lydia endured a similar inspection by a grumpy vestal and feared dismemberment or exile, as opposed to my simple unease.

Alicia tried to come to the rescue. "Beata, let's sit over here. We have wine and glasses."

"No, no. You young people have some, though."

Kinsworth asked me about my motives in building the temple. Was it merely a garden folly or had I harbored higher thoughts? Did I intend to honor Her or myself?

How would it be maintained over the years? She looked at me sharply as she awaited answers. Kinsworth could think of no other such shrine in the New World, and the ones in the Old were now mere piles of stone.

After a long silence, she said that I must establish a proper path from the main road with a handrail for the supplicants. They would soon be coming. I felt she was now on my side.

I asked, "What sort of initiation ritual is needed?"

Her voice became a raspy whisper. "Nothing formal. The mountain animals will come, large cats first, smelling around and spraying. Then, a bear or two might wander by, many curious deer, serpents in the summer and eventually all the smaller animals. They will take the word back. I can already see their scat from recent forays. See, over there and there." She pointed to some little brown piles on the outside of the courtyard.

"So it's already open and going?" I asked.

"Yes. Can't you feel it? It may take years to get up to full strength, though."

"Richard is due back from India next week, and I thought I would have his welcoming party here, as a sort of double-duty ceremony. Light refreshments, only. No grilled sausages."

"That is wise. May I come?"

With that, she motioned Alicia to accompany her back to the main road, resuming her broken military stride. I had not confessed to either of them the great change that had happened to me.

Richard sensed something, however, on his third day at home. He had finished his doctors' appointments and trips to the pharmacy, and his cough was already improving. We were eating a breakfast of his perfectly cooked, lace-free eggs and crisp bacon on the terrace facing the mountain. The temple roof shone with majesty above the piñons and junipers. After the last cups of coffee, Richard observed that I was somehow different.

"Well, a year can take its toll," I responded.

"Not in your appearance, something new within."

"A touch better, higher, more enlightened?"

"Now you're making fun of me. You speak more slowly, choosing your words. You know something we others don't."

"Can you guess what that might be?"

He considered as we walked back to the temple, his arm over my shoulder. Had the goddess rewarded me with a lottery jackpot? Had a new car materialized by itself in the driveway? Or, in keeping with the antique period, a bronze chariot? Could I now make it rain on a summer afternoon? Had the Tinos widow given in and deeded over the shuttered house? Was I going to live forever, with no new wrinkles? What was it?

I resisted telling him, thinking I might lessen my power or cancel it entirely. The reception for the temple was to be that afternoon, so I would wait to see if friends could discern what had come upon me.

There were twenty people on the temple forecourt. A young man had been hired to keep their glasses full of white wine until it got dark. The woodland sounds of a bassoon drifted above, from a musical neighbor who had offered his talents for the occasion. Alicia had put together a table of sweetmeats and canapés; as I had promised Kinsworth, there were no grilled meats, only thin slices of vegetables, deviled eggs, ground pastes on gluten-free crackers and pickled oddities.

The groups of guests made long shadows in the setting sun, and I felt as if I flew above them unnoticed, soaring high and swooping low over them. I could see the me below talking to the sharp-eyed Kinsworth, who pointed her cane up, following my flight like an artillery sergeant.

"Odd, that magpie up there," she said. "Very unlike them to be so near people." If anyone of the group could figure it out, Kinsworth could.

"I've noticed him around for several weeks now," I said on the terrace.

"*Her*, I would have thought. Plundering those deviled eggs for her fledglings."

We turned to other subjects. Keeping the bird mind and my own separate and discrete was still disconcerting for me—the one above dealing with wind eddies and landing techniques, while the one aground chatted to the guests. This bird being had come to life in my awareness in a bright flash one morning as I was sweeping leaves from the temple courtyard. I suppose it was what people call a thunderbolt. There were now two living beings sharing a single brain, a bird and a person. I could feel the two entities maneuvering about in my head, wary of their new acquaintance.

There had been some accidents in the first days. The bird crashed into a post while I, earthbound, belabored a long joke for Alicia. I stumbled down some familiar steps when the bird above took a bravura turn in a gust of wind.

On several occasions, Richard looked up at the circling magpie. He might discover the truth in time. He would be thrilled when he knew, claiming justification for his long-held belief in the workings of the netherworld. I could see him asking me to swoop down again and then clapping his hands in delight as I brushed a tail feather across his head.

"I wonder if that bird is a new sign?" he asked.

"I shouldn't think so," I replied.

"Why not? He's always here, circling over us."

"Dr. Kinsworth thinks it is a she."

"I'll keep a close eye on *her*, then."

Darkness became terrifying for me as my bird-self hid away from predators in the night, remaining still as stone on the branch of a thick spruce. Terror was a new dimension in the nights of my formerly quiet life. While Richard made slight snoring sounds, I awoke in the early hours in a terrible dread of a killer with talons gliding in slow circles near my branch, sensing its hidden meal a few feet away. What would happen to me in bed if my bird self were killed outside by an owl in the night?

Last spring when her slow voice, a strange double-tongued voice, posed the question from above the temple, I answered, *How about a time with wings?* In the boundless hours between dreams and sunlight, everyone has wished to fly. It was an obvious but flippant answer. If I were to hear that fearsome voice again—a voice that frightened the robins into full flight— and given another choice, I would suggest that several dozen of the gold coins would suffice, a mere few from the many thousands that lie scattered willy-nilly across the ocean floor near her granite ruins on the Lydian shore.

A Crescent of Easels

I had two hours before the next class during which eighteen sophomore students expected to hear from me the secrets of oil painting on a large canvas. It was spring, the weather in Austin getting hotter and the bluebonnets on the mall were already fading to brown as we approached the end of the semester.

I thought that a swim in the apartment house pool would recharge me and give me the stamina for the long studio class. Ten minutes later I pulled my vintage Mercedes sedan, a well-traveled survivor from my army years in Germany, into the parking slot for Apartment 4B. The cast-iron mailbox was bulging, so full that the mailman had not properly closed the cover. Inside were a handful of envelopes, bills and mailers, bound with a rubber band. I put the packet into my canvas briefcase on the hall table and quickly changed into swimming trunks. There was not enough time to read mail and swim forty laps as well. I would open the day's letters when I got the students started on their paintings.

I returned to the campus energized and ready for them. I said to the class, "Everybody pick the telling, perfect color and paint your plumb line on the canvas." Their resultant versions of a plumb line were as many as there were students—the green one, thin and wobbly, fearfully dividing the canvas and a strong black one, almost exactly plumb, three inches wide, and an earth-red variation done in small angled strokes, top to bottom, like the petrified backbone of a long-dead amphibian. The most promising student,

Margaretta Dittrick had painted hers from bottom to top, confident and wide, leaving gaps of varying widths on the way up. Her painting already had rhythm and direction.

The plumb line was the literal spine of my method for teaching beginners to approach a large canvas, an idea I found in writings by Matisse. The line violated the virginity of the white canvas, denying the terrible strength of its purity and giving the painter a place from which to work. Divide and conquer. From here on, life would be getting better, Matisse said. I read the passage aloud at the beginning of each semester, as well as his other comments about the sense of verticality being so vital to a canvas.

I liked teaching, but I wondered if students could really be taught to paint, or was this ability in the bones, like perfect pitch. Margaretta had it, whatever it was, and probably did not need a minute of my class. Drawing could be taught, I believed, but not painting itself. This notion was heretical at my university art department, but I would continue teaching students to not quite paint and not quite become artists. It gave me a way to be at the easel until I could paint every day on my own, make art my life.

Margaretta was in love with me, a bad situation for an instructor, but nothing would ever come of it, despite her pleadings. I told her that I was a bachelor and lived alone because I preferred the solitary life. This was not the entire truth, but there was certainly no room in my life for a young girl, however talented and promising.

She placed her easel at the end the large semi-circle so the other students could not hear well when I discussed her canvas. She had tried everything to pique my interest—slyly exposing her breasts, showing sweetness, boldness, neediness, harshness, even silence. She bombarded me with obscure quotes from art historians, questions about a particular color, salacious offers and, several times, gushes of tears. I responded with kind, firm rejections, again and again. If obsession was the guarantee for success in art, she would surely be the next O'Keeffe.

Through it all, she painted extraordinary canvases, one after the other, getting better and better. Following the exposed bosom business, she filled a panel with breasts and nipples of so many shapes that they mingled and merged into circles within circles, a mammary-invaded universe. After we talked about the correct color for illustrating passionate love, she mixed eighty shades of crimson and scarlet into small sharp cutting lines, as if a razor blade had slashed the painting, letting multi-colored blood come through and dribble down. She could take an event or idea from her own life and convert it into an exhilarating pattern, a matrix upon which to build the finished canvas. If we could complete our academic term together without open revolt, or mental breakdown on either side, she would be well on her way into an art career. Her junior year, the following year, another professor could take the brunt of the attack as her laser love refocused on him, no doubt an equally unhappy target.

At the previous session, the entire class discussed the idea for this day's painting. The motif was to be expressed through the use of the plumb line, growing out from it, embellishing it, or perhaps replacing it. We considered unhappiness, madness, elation, Wall Street, childbirth and grief, but finally settled upon the motif of urbanity. The students were to paint what it was to be in the middle of a city today, expressing parts of the loneliness and the collective joy equally. I would let them proceed on their own for the first hour, then slowly walk along the crescent of easels, commenting, suggesting, questioning, sometimes actually demonstrating with paint on the student's canvas. At the end of the crescent there would be the inevitable confrontation with Margaretta. But, before that transit, for the first hour of painting, I would have the time to look through my letters.

The top envelope was from the gallery in Santa Fe that handled my work. It reported the sale of two paintings, check enclosed, and asked that I provide more paintings with the same motif, ASAP. This was the best sort of mail. Maybe my teaching days were coming to their end, no more needy Margarettas in my future. It had been a dream of long ago, when a life of art and love in faraway Morocco seemed possible.

The next letter was from the Army National Guard, notifying me that I had completed my six-year service obligation, which consisted of two years of active duty in Germany, followed by four of inactive duty at home. A handsome full-color Honorable Discharge certificate on card stock documenting this had already been mailed under separate cover, signed by the commanding general.

The third letter was from my mother, who wrote of Dad's continuing decline and the month-old news that the April Bird Census had been a great success, despite the steering committee's grave questions over her solo sighting of a male Phainopepla, with his glossy blue-black feathers. Much too far from the Mexican seacoast, they insinuated. A strong woman, my mother gave battle even in the placid world of birding.

In my mail there were also an invitation to an art exhibit at a local Austin gallery, an electric bill, a gas bill, some advertising flyers, a solicitation from the Mattachine Society and one last envelope, from Wisconsin, from Melanie Follum. I recognized her curvilinear script and wondered once again if the flowing tracery resembled more the whiplash or the spider web.

Melanie sent me regular letters on the details of her life together with Eric—how good-looking he still was and how he had gained so little weight, unlike his brothers. She described the dinners she cooked for Eric and how they adored their time alone. Her unwritten but actual message was that if love was the Great War, she was the victor. Eric was now hers, all hers. Her open friendliness suggested that the weapons were buried, bygones forgotten. A true victor would not have to crow so loud nor walk so nervously along the frontiers, again and again.

They both worried, she often wrote, that I was still alone after all these years. I never received a letter from Eric himself, and our stormy parting night years ago the last we had touched. I presumed Melanie monitored Eric's outgoing mail closely and I often thought of him as Dumas's masked man, deep in a French dungeon, straining to hear a sympathetic sound through the thick masonry walls.

Eric and Melanie's marriage ceremony had been held without my participation while I was teaching at art school. Every six or seven months thereafter postcards arrived from their vacation destinations, which were mostly music-centered conventions around the world. Afterwards, Melanie sent snapshots of the happy couple, both of them smiling on a bridge in Toronto, arm in arm on a palm-lined street in Los Angeles or in the midst of a restaurant filled with other professorial couples. All this was to provide me solid evidence that their life was happy in the melodious northland. However, what the photographs said to me was quite different—how Eric had grown even more handsome in our years apart, his look of poetic melancholy more pronounced as well.

Melanie's message this time comprised only three sentences in her florid script on the back of a printed card. She wrote:

> *We think of you so often, Eric and I, and wish you could be*
> *with us for Eric's conducting of the Spring Cantata,*
> *the full St. Olaf Philharmonic and the 100-voice university chorus.*
> *A secular cantata by J.S. Bach—if you don't know it.*
> *Love as always, Melanie.*

The card itself was a printed invitation with yellow daisies in the corners, to a baptism at the Redeemer Lutheran Church in late February, sent on three months late. The child's name was Mary Tangier Follum, their beloved daughter.

Melanie surely did not understand the subterranean messages to me from Eric in the card, like secrets written in disappearing ink. Tangier was to have been Eric's and my love destination, where all our hopes for happiness would materialize in an open-windowed, earthen cottage on the edge of town. All would have been possible on the Moroccan shore.

Eric's choice of Bach's Spring Cantata was not a coincidence. It echoed a sensuous summer night when two men in uniform side by side at the back of a German concert hall listened to Bach's choral crescendos, higher and higher, and a forbidden love between them sparked into life. It was a love now fading but not quite extinguished, thin curlicues of smoke hovering over the embers. I hoped on windy nights in the birch woods of Wisconsin there was another clandestine, pulsating red glow.

It was time to start my stroll along the crescent of easels, encouraging the work on this canvas, drawing a corrected line on that. *You must think of the canvas as a whole, not as an accidental meeting of pieces.* I lost my focus at the fifth easel, gazing into a painting of solid blue, its entire plumb line covered. The student waited patiently for my commentary while my thoughts rode high above the blue painting to an image fixed forever in my mind.

Was it possible to journey back in time, perhaps on a magical small Tabriz, to that anger-filled night years ago when Eric and I parted? We had chosen to walk away from the dilemma rather than solving it. If it was not too late to trowel plaster into that gaping crack, to make the wall once more smooth to the touch, where did I need to start?

How to Buy a Turkish Rug

1890. A mercantile drama for two spoken male voices, the baritone in top
hat and tails and the tenor wearing gallibaya and fez,
singing intermittently, with musical interludes and backgrounds,
a deep woman's singing voice for when the grandmothers are mentioned
and a small woman's chorus for when the women weavers
or the unmarried daughters are mentioned.

Good morning. Mr. Selçut, I presume? I need a rug.

    The Selçut Paradise of Carpets has the most beautiful rugs. You have
    visited our city before?

Many times—a lovely, lovely city.

    A businessman, then? Here for the plunge of the lira? Or for the
    precious slabs of our up-country marble?

Only a holiday sea voyage.

    On the ship with black sails at our city docks?

The same. The rug I'm looking for is large…hiding from us somewhere in
these rooms.

    Have no fear, the Selçut sons will prise it out. How large must it be?

Sixteen—seventeen feet long.

    For the many-roomed house on a high hill?

A small house in the valley, actually, with a bare wood floor.

Look at these, my friend. Finely knotted, rich colors, silks and wools—
the largest selection in all Constantinople.

I look for pale colors and faded patterns.

But Turkey is famous for her indigo purples and vibrant reds.

My floor asks for pale yellows and soft russets.

I am sad to report that very plain rugs might cost many dollars more.

Despite the demand for purples and reds?

It is the curious world of carpets, Effendi.

I understand. What about this one?

From Milas—Anatolian colors and patterns not popular with our
best collectors. Seventeen feet, however.

And you ask notably less for such unpopular colors and patterns?

Any carpet from Milas is so very rare.

What is the asking price?

Turmoil reigns in Anatolia while we stay behind the city walls.
Smoke fills the horizon there and the women weavers are on the edge,
as you say. Eight hundred dollars.

My gracious. For unpopular colors?

Only the oldest grandmothers with gnarled fingers remember these
designs.

I must look elsewhere. Eight hundred is vastly beyond my budget.

Budget? What is this budget?

It means the logical matching of your asking price to the money at hand.

How very odd. Can it be wise for rare art?

I buy all goods with a budget.

Six hundred dollars, then, to give the gentleman from the great black
ship a nice reduction for his … budget.

The great ship will sail soon and many merchants called out to my carriage.

Six hundred, then—the very best price. My daughters will lose their
patrimony. Let us roll out this beauty all the way to admire.

May I make a counter-offer?

Give and take is the Turkish way, Effendi.

Eighty dollars. *My* very best price.

> *Star of Allah! Such miserliness will bring disgrace to my innocent
> daughters.*

But that's what the budget says.

> *What a troublesome devil is your budget. But here comes the servant
> with the mint tea, to bring sanity to our dealings. Let us sit.*

Sir, eighty dollars is a generous sum the world over, no matter how much tea
we drink.

> *Can you not hear the upstairs coughing of my bedridden grand-
> mother, who loves so dearly her large rugs from Milas?*

Even now, my own church-going grandmother waits on a bare floor to have
her feet warmed.

> *Cruel times abide here in Turkey, kind sir. We ask only for basic
> goods…once-milled flour, small potatoes, thin soups.*

If there is to be no progress, Mr. Selçut, I should visit the more agreeable,
smaller establishments. The friendly ones who waved.

> *Four hundred, then. The absolute very best price.*

Imagine how happy this rug will be with the western sunlight falling across
its well-knotted borders. Eighty dollars is serious money—a month's wages
for an American family.

> *Not along the Bosporus. My daughters will weep—for them no
> husbands possible.*

It is foolish for me to squander the hard-won coin of the west.

> *I assure you, Effendi, my women will fill the Sea of Marmara with
> their salty tears if so few of your hard-won coins come their way.*

There are few minutes left. Eighty dollars and your beautiful Milas carpet
will grace my western floor

> *Two hundred. Shipping, of course, extra.*

The budget says eighty.

> *Even Satan cannot smile at this number. Now, with my daughters on
> their knees, you must bring us more.*

Very well. Ninety-five dollars.

Severed hand of Fatima!

Gracious me. Is that the ship's bell?

Two hundred…and no Selçut evening meals for a year.

Cash, my friend. Crinkly dollar bills, asking for life in the Empire—enough for dozens of Bosporus red-fish meals and many shiny rings for every daughter.

Such pillage will undo the age-old beauty of Byzantium.

I ought to look at this rug from the other direction.

Stand here and gaze back at the sheen, breathe in the aroma of the
Aegean. Two hundred and my sons will weigh it for shipping.

I will come all the way up to one hundred dollars—to cover shipping to the invader's doorstep, taxes, duties, port charges and all the other charges, of course.

Aeieee! Lest my cousin merchants deride, a small bit more.

One hundred and two dollars, shipping included.

Ah, well…the Selçut clan must crumble to the west. My first son will
draw up the papers…and the Sultan asks a small recompense to
repair his docks from your sharp ships.

In the past a gentleman expected small gifts from the better merchants of Constantinople. Two prayer rugs, perhaps, in your fabled deep reds. Easily slipped inside the larger rug.

How low you ask us to bow. With fondness I look back to yesterday's
customers, agreeable sisters from the Minnesota. But, we Selçuts
are big-hearted and thank you and from her narrow bed my
grandmother waves her thin hand, her battles lost.

I wonder, kind sir, if there was a lower sum like fifty dollars that I did not see? Was I unwise to start so high?

Only Allah knows such secrets. As you cross the salty Sea of Marma-
ra, drinking devil-waters on the high deck, the wind in your sails,
remember with a tear the Selçut family—our now-diminished
inventory and the years of spare table ahead.

Thanks

It gives me pleasure to acknowledge the people who helped me write this collection of stories. First, thanks to the group of friends who listened with patience over several summers as I read the newly-written pages after dinners in Lake City, Colorado. It was at Shelley McGehee's house by the river with Doug Bland, Walter Cooper, Billy Halsted, Wayne Bladh, John Fincher, Judith Cloud and others, who kindly allowed me to read them aloud. And thanks, also, to Felicia Eppley who brought by the book of Chinese poems with the idea for *Deer Park*. Later, when I finished the first draft, Wendy Schiller took her sharp, copy-editing pencil to the stories, bringing order and clarity. And last, thanks to Jim and Carl at Sunstone Press, for their continued support of my work.